The Protein Group

BY TAMMY KENNINGTON

The Child's World

Published by The Child's World®
1980 Lookout Drive • Mankato, MN 56003-1705
800-599-READ • www.childsworld.com

Acknowledgments
The Child's World®: Mary Berendes, Publishing Director
Red Line Editorial: Editorial direction
The Design Lab: Design
Amnet: Production
Photographs ©: Front cover: FoodIcons; BrandX Pictures; FoodIcons,
3, 12, 16; BrandX Pictures, 3, 10; Hong Vo/Shutterstock Images, 4;
choosemyplate.gov, 5; ComStock, 6; Africa Studio/Shutterstock Images,
8; Monkey Business Images/Shutterstock Images, 9; fredericofoto/
Shutterstock Images, 11; El Nariz/Shutterstock Images, 13; Catalin
Petolea/Shutterstock Images, 14; Nitr/Shutterstock Images, 17; Milleflore
Images/Shutterstock Images, 19; bonchan/Shutterstock Images, 21

ISBN: 978-1623236052
LCCN: 2013931394

Printed in the United States of America
Mankato, MN
July, 2013
PA02178

ABOUT THE AUTHOR

Tammy Kennington holds a bachelor of arts degree in elementary education and has earned certification as a reading intervention specialist. She currently serves as a preschool director and tutors children with dyslexia and related reading disorders. Tammy lives in Colorado Springs with her husband and four children.

Table of Contents

CHAPTER ONE

Protein Pointers

You wake up in the morning to a deep, rumbling sound. *Grrrowl*. Burrowing deeper into the warm blankets, you ignore it. There it is again, except the noise is louder. *Grrrowl*. "Hey, Dad!" you yell. "Stop snoring!" *Grrrowl*. Suddenly, you realize the sound is coming from you. What is going on?

Your vibrating stomach is sending a message to your brain. "I need energy. Feed me!" Shuffling to the kitchen, you reach for your favorite cereal, Sugar Ohs.

► **Opposite page: The MyPlate guidelines tell you to fill about one-quarter of your plate with protein foods.**

▼ **Sugary cereals may be sweet, but they do not keep you full for long.**

4

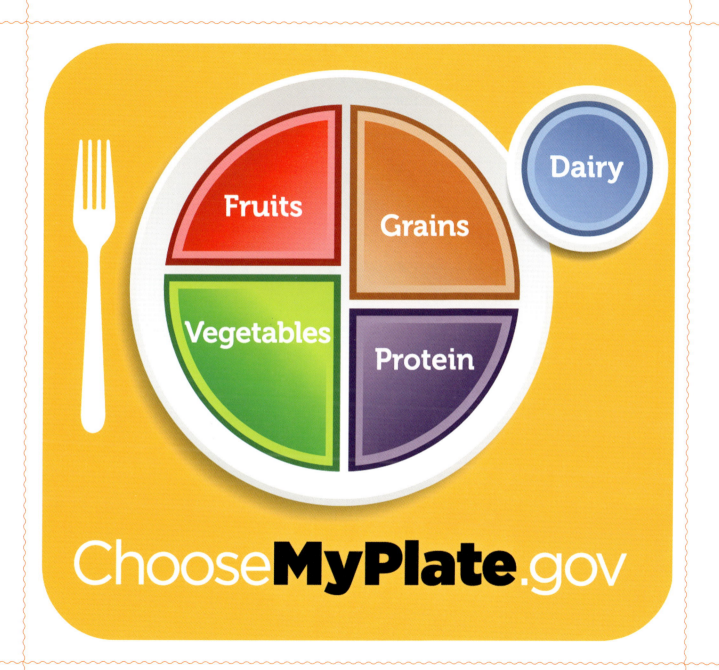

Fruits

Grains

Dairy

Vegetables

Protein

ChooseMyPlate.gov

You know eating breakfast is important, but could you choose foods that keep you fuller longer? Where can you find out more about eating healthy foods?

The MyPlate guidelines show the five food groups that make up a healthy diet: **protein**, grains, vegetables, fruits, and dairy. They illustrate what your plate, bowl, or cup should look like at every meal. MyPlate includes the protein group as an important part of healthy eating. Protein should make up about one-quarter of your plate every meal.

◄ Protein helps build strong muscles and gives your body energy.

The word *protein* can be used to describe both an **essential nutrient** and a type of food. As an essential nutrient, protein gives your body energy, builds your muscles, and keeps your **tissues** and **organs** strong and working properly. Almost half of your body is made of protein, including muscles, skin, hair, and organs. Did you know that protein repairs your skin when you have been scratched?

The body does not produce its own essential protein. You need to eat protein foods to stay fit and healthy. Although most Americans get enough protein in their diets, not all protein foods are the same. Protein foods come from animal products like meat, **poultry**, eggs, milk, and fish. Plant foods such as **legumes**, **soy**, and spinach are good sources of protein, too. Protein foods are important to a balanced diet.

▶ Opposite page: Protein foods such as chicken are part of a balanced meal.

▼ All of these foods provide your body with the protein it needs.

CHAPTER TWO

Beef, Beans, and Eating Lean

▶ Opposite page: Chicken and beef contain protein and other essential nutrients.

▼ Beans are a great source of protein.

"Am I getting enough protein?" you may wonder. According to experts, most people who eat a healthy diet get enough protein. But what should that healthy diet include? Both animal and plant foods are protein sources.

When you eat protein foods, your body breaks the protein into building blocks called **amino acids**. Amino acids help your body repair its tissues, break down foods, and grow. You must eat

protein foods to get the nine essential amino acids your body needs.

Protein foods also provide the **vitamins** and **minerals** your body needs to work properly and grow strong and healthy. Protein foods such as eggs, fish, and nuts contain B vitamins and vitamin E. These nutrients help your body fight illnesses and create and strengthen your blood. Foods such as meat, beans, and poultry have important minerals, including iron, zinc, and magnesium. These minerals help your body build bones, fight illnesses, and carry oxygen in your blood.

Eating protein foods will provide your body with all of the essential amino acids. It will also help you eat enough vitamins and minerals. Animal protein foods such as milk, meat, poultry, fish, and eggs contain high-quality protein. Plants such as legumes, nuts, grains, seeds, and soybeans also

A HAIRY SITUATION
What do your hair, teeth, fingernails, and skin have in common with horse hooves and spiders' webs? They are all made of a strong protein called keratin. Depending on which amino acids are used, keratin can be hard or soft.

contain protein. You should eat different kinds of protein foods so you get all the essential amino acids. For example, **vegetarians** must carefully pick their protein sources because they do not eat meat. Healthy options include peanut butter, beans, and tofu—a food made from the soybean plant.

Although juicy hamburgers and steaks provide your body protein, they are also high in fat. Eating

▶ **Eat a variety of protein foods to make sure you get all the essential amino acids.**

◄ **Opposite page: Eat lean meat such as chicken or turkey to avoid eating too much fat.**

types of meat with less fat is a healthy choice for everyone. Tasty, leaner options include chicken, pork, and fish. Ask your family to try grilled chicken breasts instead of steak. Make fish for dinner at least once a week. Or cook up a tasty chili with pinto and kidney beans.

► **Chili makes a protein-packed meal on a cold day.**

CHAPTER THREE

Fuel Up

Protein is an important part of a healthy diet. You should eat protein foods at every meal. Kids ages four to eight need about 4 ounces of protein every day. Girls and boys between nine and 13 years old need about 5 ounces each day. All these foods count as 1 ounce of protein:

- One egg
- One slice of turkey
- One-half of a small hamburger
- 24 almonds
- 1/4 cup cooked beans

Did you know that breakfast is the most important meal of the day? While you sleep, your body makes muscle tissue, repairs itself, and grows.

▲ **One-half of a small hamburger counts as 1 ounce of protein.**

▶ **Opposite page: A breakfast with protein foods such as eggs will keep you full until lunch.**

If you skip breakfast or choose cereals with a lot of sugar, you will not be able to concentrate in school. You may feel tired or grumpy by midmorning.

Eating protein foods at breakfast will not only boost your brainpower and energy level, but will help you feel full all morning. Take a few extra minutes before school to fuel up with protein power. Fry up an egg omelet with diced ham or sprinkle granola with nuts over your yogurt. Wash it all down with a glass of milk.

There are healthy protein foods you can eat at lunch and dinner, too. Put together a turkey sandwich with lettuce and tomato on whole-wheat bread. Spread peanut butter on a celery stick and top with raisins. Help family members grill salmon or chicken for dinner. Serve these delicious protein foods with rice and broccoli and a glass of milk.

▼ Wash down meals with a glass of milk for an extra protein punch!

► You can choose from many different types of protein foods.

EGG-CITING NEWS ABOUT POULTRY

Did you know that...

- the average chicken lays 259 eggs every year?
- a hen starts laying eggs when she is just over four months old?
- depending on the type of chicken, eggs can be brown, white, cream, or blue?
- a hard-boiled egg will spin?
- Benjamin Franklin wanted the turkey to be the national bird of the United States?

Add some fruit for dessert and you have a complete MyPlate meal!

Protein is one of the essential nutrients that everybody needs to grow and stay healthy. Following the MyPlate guidelines will help you make sure you get enough protein to power all of your activities. Eating the MyPlate way helps make a healthy you!

Hands-on Activity: Egg-cellent Eggs

Did you know that one egg contains 12 percent of the protein you need each day? Eggs can be prepared in hundreds of ways. Find an adult and make this delicious egg drop soup recipe together.

What You'll Need:

A medium-sized pot, an egg, two 16-ounce cans of chicken broth, cornstarch, a serving bowl, a spoon

Directions:

1. First, in the pot, mix the two cans of chicken broth with 1 tablespoon of cornstarch.
2. Then, heat the ingredients on the stovetop at medium heat.
3. Next, crack the egg into a small mixing bowl. When the soup is warm, stir the egg into the broth mixture.
4. Lastly, remove from the heat.

Serve the soup in a small bowl and enjoy!

Glossary

amino acids (uh-MEE-no AS-idz): Amino acids are the small building blocks your body gets from protein. There are nine essential amino acids.

essential (ee-SEN-chul): Something that is essential is necessary or important. Protein is an essential nutrient.

legumes (LEG-yoomz): Legumes are members of a plant family with seed pods that split on both sides. Beans, peas, lentils, and peanuts are legumes.

minerals (MIN-er-ulz): Minerals are substances—such as calcium, magnesium, and iron—found in foods that your body needs to function. People can get some of their daily minerals from protein.

nutrient (NOO-tree-ent): A nutrient is any substance that feeds or nourishes a body. Protein is an essential nutrient.

organs (OR-gunz): Organs are parts of the body that have specific jobs. Your lungs, stomach, and heart are organs.

poultry (POL-tree): Poultry are birds that people raise for eggs or meat. Poultry is a good source of protein.

protein (PRO-teen): Protein is a part of food that provides energy and contains building blocks used by the whole body. Protein is found in meat, beans, nuts, and seeds.

soy (soy): Soy foods are foods made from soybeans. Soy is a good protein choice for vegetarians.

tissues (TISH-yooz): Tissues are made up of groups of similar cells that form a part or all of an organ in your body. Protein helps build and repair tissues.

vegetarians (vej-uh-TAIR-ee-unz): Vegetarians are people who eat only plants and plant products and sometimes eggs or dairy products. Vegetarians eat beans, seeds, and nuts instead of meat to get protein.

vitamins (VYE-tuh-minz): Vitamins are substances found in foods that help your body stay healthy. Vitamins are found in protein foods.

To Learn More

BOOKS

Haduch, Bill. *Food Rules! The Stuff You Munch, Its Crunch, Its Punch, and Why You Sometimes Lose Your Lunch.* New York: Dutton Children's Books, 2001.

Miller, Edward. *The Monster Health Book: A Guide to Eating Healthy, Being Active, and Feeling Great for Monsters and Kids!* New York: Holiday House, 2006.

WEB SITES

Visit our Web site for links about protein: **childsworld.com/links**

Note to Parents, Teachers, and Librarians: We routinely verify our Web links to make sure they are safe and active sites. So encourage your readers to check them out!

Index

FROM SINAI TO JERUSALEM

The Wanderings of the Holy Ark

Leen and Kathleen Ritmeyer

carta

Illustrations by Leen Ritmeyer on pp. 6–7, 8–9, 10–11, 12, 14,
16–17, 18 (below), 19, 22 (below), 24, 28–29, 30, 32–33, 36–37,
40 (below), 41 (upper), 44 (below), 45, 46, 47, 48 (below),
49 (below), 50–51, 52–53, 54–55, 56, 58-59, 60–61,
62 (below center), 62–63, 64, 67, 68–69, 70, 71 (below)

All others Carta, Jerusalem

First edition 2000
Copyright © 2000 Carta,
The Israel Map and Publishing Company Ltd.

Designed and produced by Carta, Jerusalem
Editor: Barbara Ball
Artwork: Leen Ritmeyer
Additional artwork:
Elisabeth Nesis

ISBN 965-220-434-X

Printed in Israel.

INTRODUCTION

The wonderful story of the Wanderings of the Ark has fascinated Bible readers for generations. It is one of the most exciting events recorded by man and vividly described in the Bible.

Various routes have been suggested for the Ark, whose journey spanned more than a thousand years, and all texts, as does this one, still carry question marks. For better understanding, we have provided a number of photographs of the various regions through which the Ark passed, from its construction by Bezaleel in the wilderness of Sinai to its final destination in the Holy of Holies of Solomon's Temple.

Scholars and artists have long grappled with the intricacies of the biblical descriptions. Over the centuries many proposals have been made in both word and picture for the Tabernacle and its artifacts. The authors offer a wide-ranging and possible scenario with the region as a backdrop, by combining original photographs, interpretive drawings based on Scripture, and reconstructions based on archaeological evidence together with contemporary finds.

The brief narrative with its biblical references focuses, in the main, on the central illustration of each chapter.

A rich source of reference, this handy volume provides a fount of knowledge accumulated over time for the enjoyment of the reader. Scholars, teachers and students may use it as a stepping stone for further reading and research.

Bible quotations are from the Authorized (King James) Version because the majesty and simplicity of its language are made to relate one of mankind's most wondrous experiences.

Contents

The Sojourn in Sinai and the Building of the Tabernacle and the Holy Ark

The Mountains of Sinai

Mount Sinai, it is believed, is where Moses spoke to God and received the Law on two stone tablets. Here, too, he was instructed how to make the Ark of the Covenant to hold the testimony or the two tablets of the Law and also how to build the Tabernacle, the movable enclosure of which the Ark was the focal point.

As to the identification of this mountain with the mountain of God, all that Scripture tells us is that after the children of Israel had come out of Egypt, they left Rephidim, came to Sinai, pitched themselves in the wilderness, and "there Israel camped before the mount" (Ex. 19.2). Rephidim can almost certainly be identified with Wadi Feiran, a long lush valley that leads into the peninsula from the coastal plain.

Approaching the Sinai desert from the coast, one is struck by the imposing forms of the Sinai Massif rising out of the surrounding plateau. Claims have been made for some of the other higher peaks in the range to be identified as the original Mount Sinai. Some of these could well fit the description in Deuteronomy 1.2: "There are eleven days' journey from Horeb (Sinai) by the way of mount Seir unto Kadesh-barnea." However, other essential requirements described in Scripture are missing.

Exodus tells us that Moses brought the people out of the camp to meet with God "and they stood at the nether part of the mount" (19.17), nesessitating a single mountain, not part of a range. In addition, the surroundings at the base of none of the other peaks, such as Serbal, allow for the encampment of a large body of people. Furthermore, they were to "set bounds" about the mount (Ex. 19.12), to stop the people from climbing or touching it. Most graphically, it is recorded that when the people saw the mount quaking "they removed, and stood afar off" (Ex. 20.18).

At Ras Safsafeh, the peak at the northern extremity of Jebel Musa, one can best visualize the events of the giving of the Law. The long approach to this site would allow for the occurrence of the various incidents during Moses' seven ascents to the mountain. The foot of this dramatic peak is lined with mounds that appear as a blockage for access. Most convincing of all is the wide, surrounding plain of Er Rahah, which provided ample space for the terrified Israelites to retreat from the spectacle of the smoking mountain.

Although later tradition had chosen the "true Mount Sinai" to be the high peak of Jebel Musa, with the Monastery of Saint Catherine at its base, it was actually Ras Safsafeh that the early Byzantines identified with biblical Horeb.

Moses and the burning bush, from a wall painting in the synagogue at Dura-Europos, Syria, third century.

5

A view of Jebel Musa, one of the peaks of the Sinai massif which has traditionally been identified as Mount Sinai.

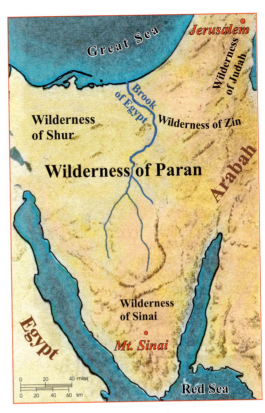

Map of the wildernesses in the Sinai peninsula.

Nineteenth century engraving of Robinson's Arch in Jerusalem, named after the American scholar.

Edward Robinson (1794–1863), the eminent American biblical scholar, wrote of his first view of this place: "[The plain] terminated at the distance of more than a mile by the bold and awful front of Horeb (Ras Safsafeh) rising perpendicularly in frowning majesty from twelve to fifteen hundred feet in height. It was a scene of solemn grandeur wholly unexpected, and such as we had never seen, and the associations, which at the moment rushed upon our minds, were almost overwhelming" (Biblical Researches in Palestine, Boston, 1841, pp. 190–191).

The Tabernacle and the Camp of Israel

The encampment of the Israelites in the plain of Er-Rahah must have presented a truly dramatic scene. As soon as the Tabernacle was set up, it became the focal point of an immense camp. In 1868-69 Captain H. S. Palmer carried out an ordnance survey of the entire Sinai Peninsula. His measurements showed "that the space extending from the base of the mountain to the watershed or crest of the plain is large enough to have accommodated the entire host of the Israelites, estimated at 2 million souls, with an allowance of about a square yard for each individual."

The four-sided camp stood on the plain in the divinely prescribed order, with the stern jagged granite peak from which God spoke as its backdrop. Each side of the encampment was shared by three tribes under the standard of the leading tribe for that group. Thus, Judah, Issachar and Zebulun camped on the east side under the standard of Judah. Reuben, Simeon and Gad were on the south side under the standard of Reuben. On the west were Ephraim, Manasseh and Benjamin under the standard of Ephraim, while on the north were the tribes of Dan, Asher and Naphtali under the standard of Dan.

Within this sea of tents was a thin row that belonged to the priestly families. On the east were the tents of Moses and Aaron, while on the south was the family of Kohath. The family of Gershon encamped on the west, while the family of Merari had their row of tents in the north. All these surrounded the Tabernacle, over which rested a pillar of cloud that shaded the entire camp from the intense desert sun (Ps. 105.39).

The children of Israel remained in this valley for a year while the Tabernacle, its furnishings and the priestly garments were being made. Exodus 40.17 tells us that the Tabernacle was "reared up" in the first month

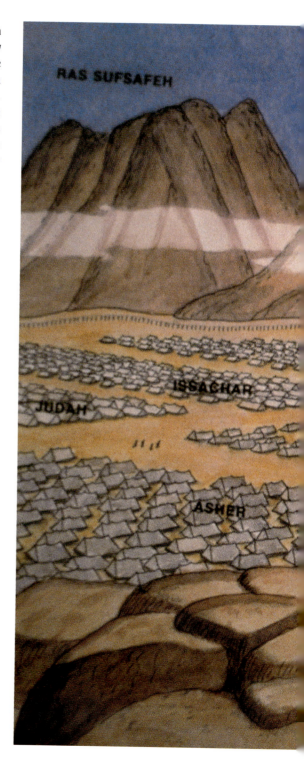

of the second year of the Israelites' stay in Sinai, whereas Numbers 10.11-12 gives us the date on which they left this spot, the twentieth day of the second month. Sometime during these seven weeks, as recorded in Numbers 2, the Israelites were transformed from a shapeless mass of people into a nation whose progress through the desert was prescribed down to the minutest detail and whose discipline would be the envy of any military commander. From a scene such as this the Ark commenced its wanderings.

An artist's depiction of the encampment of Israel around the Tabernacle at the foot of Mount Horeb.

JEBEL MUSA

ZEBULUN
REUBEN
SIMEON
AARON
MOSES
KOHATH
MERARI
TABERNACLE
GERSHON
BENJAMIN
DAN

The Tabernacle

Moses was commanded to make the Tabernacle according to the pattern shown to him on the mount (Ex. 25.40). As the tents of the children of Israel were portable, so the Sanctuary that God commanded to be made for Him could also be dismantled and re-erected.

The journey from Mount Sinai to the Promised Land takes only a few weeks, but because of disobedience to God's commands the journey was to last forty years. Long after the Israelites settled in the Promised Land, this portable sanctuary was a visible reminder of their former nomadic existence in Sinai. It was

Model of the Tabernacle, produced in England in about 1950.

to serve as a focal point for national worship at Gibeon even after David had brought the Ark up into the City of David (1 Chron. 16.39) more than 1,000 years later.

The *shittah* (pl. *shittim*) tree, or acacia, was the wood from which the basic frame of the Tabernacle was made (Ex. 26.15). This tree, though rare in Israel, is the most common one found in the Sinai. In fact, the name Sinai probably derives from the Hebrew *seneh*, a name given to another variety of acacia.

The materials used to make and furnish the Tabernacle were provided by the Israelites, who had been given gold and silver jewelry and clothing by the Egyptians. The weight of gold used in the making of the Sanctuary was 29 talents and 730 shekels. The amount of silver employed was 100 talents and 1,730 shekels. The experience gained working on Egyptian building projects must surely have produced many skilled craftsmen for this project from among the Israelites.

The Tabernacle was surrounded by an open court formed of sixty pillars with silver capitals. Each pillar stood in a brass socket and was secured by cords and tent pins made of brass. On this framework, which measured 100 by 50 cubits (172 by 86 feet or 52.50 m by 26.25 m), hung curtains of fine white linen. The entrance to the court was via a curtain of fine linen interwoven with blue, purple and scarlet supported by four pillars.

Within the open court stood the Altar of Burnt Offering and the Laver. The Laver stood between the Altar of Burnt Offering and the Tabernacle entrance. Here the priests washed before performing their priestly duties.

The Tabernacle itself was made of boards of *shittim* wood overlaid with gold along three of its sides and was 30 cubits (52 feet or 15.75 m) long and 10 cubits (17 feet or 5.25 m) wide. These boards rested in silver sockets and were further held upright by bars that traversed each of the three sides. Cords attached to the ground with brass pins further ensured its stability. The entrance to the Tabernacle was on the east side facing the Brazen Altar and the Laver. Here five pillars supported a curtain similar to that at the entrance to the outer court. Apart from this entranceway, the entire structure was covered with four layers of coverings. Fine linen, again interwoven with blue, purple and scarlet, formed the ceiling of the Tabernacle. This was followed with a covering made of goat's hair, then ram's skins dyed red and, finally, what is most frequently translated as badgers' skins (Hebrew *tachashim*, which derives from the root for "silence").

Inside the Tabernacle, a veil separated the Holy, which was 20 cubits long and 10 wide, from the Most Holy (10 by 10 cubits) into which only the High Priest could enter once a year on the Day of Atonement. In the Holy stood a Table for the Shewbread, the Golden Lampstand and the Altar of Incense. Beyond the veil stood the Ark of the Covenant.

"And thou shalt make boards for the tabernacle of shittim wood standing up" (Ex. 26.15). The acacia or shittah tree is among the most common species found in Sinai.

The Ark of the Covenant

Scripture reveals that it was the Ark that God first commanded to be made. The rest of the furnishings of the Tabernacle came afterwards. Like the light that was created in Genesis (1.3) to shine upon a dark world before God created the rest of the elements, so the primacy of the Ark in the sequence of the making of the Tabernacle pointed forward to the pre-eminence of Messiah in God's purpose.

The Ark consisted of a rectangular chest, 2.5 cubits long by 1.5 cubits wide (4.3 by 2.6 ft. or 1.31 by 0.79 m), made of acacia wood and overlaid inside and out with gold (Ex. 25.10,11). An ornamental border that went around the top of the Ark is called in Scripture the "crown of gold." The lid of the Ark was also made of pure gold and was known as the "mercy seat." Rising out of the two sides of this mercy seat and beaten out of the same piece of gold were the Cherubim, winged figures whose faces looked towards the mercy seat.

When the Ark was first made, it contained only the two tablets of stone on which God had engraved the Ten Commandments (Ex. 25.16). From the Book of Hebrews (9.4), however, we learn that two other items were also placed inside the Ark: a golden pot filled with manna, the food God provided for the Israelites during their forty years in the wilderness, and the almond rod that budded miraculously, proving that the selection of Aaron as High Priest was divinely appointed. This record does not specify when these two items were added but would indicate that it was at some time during the wilderness journey. Just before his death (Deut. 31.24-26), Moses was commanded to have a scroll of laws (probably the Pentateuch) written and to place it either inside the Ark or by its side (it is difficult to determine which from the text).

Two staves, also made of *shittim* wood and covered with gold, were slotted through golden

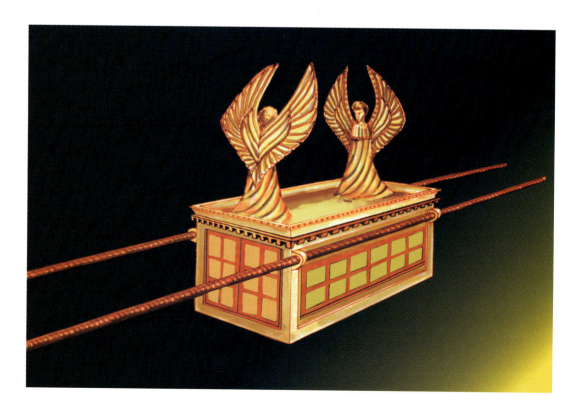

Drawing of the Ark of the Covenant.

12

rings so that the Ark could be moved from one place to another. Scripture does not give the length of these staves, but a Talmudic reference (*Yoma* 54a) states that they were 10 cubits (17.2 ft. or 5.25 m) long. They could not have been longer as the Ark of the Covenant with the staves would not have fitted inside the Holy of Holies, which measured 10 cubits square.

In the Temple of Solomon, the Most Holy was sometimes called the Oracle (Hebrew *dvir*, from the root "to speak"). It was from here that God communicated with Israel, as he said to Moses "and there I will meet with thee and I will commune with thee from above the mercy-seat, from between the two cherubim which are upon the ark of the testimony, of all things which I will give thee in commandment unto the children of Israel" (Ex. 25.22). Apart from Moses, this place of "thick darkness" (1 Kings 8.12) was entered only once a year by the High Priest on the Day of Atonement when he sprinkled blood upon and before the mercy seat, having first placed a censer of incense before the Ark "that he die not" (Lev. 16.13).

God indicated to the Israelites that they were to march by taking up the cloud that covered the Tabernacle. They then journeyed to where the divine led. The order in which they moved was also divinely appointed. First went the camp of Judah, then the sons of Gershon and Merari carrying the various items that made up the Tabernacle structure with the curtains and hangings for the court. The camp of the Reubenites followed. The Kohathites then set forward carrying the vessels of the Sanctuary, including the Ark. The Levites carried the Ark on their shoulders by means of the two long staves. The staves were left in the rings so as always to be ready at a moment's notice for the next journey. The camp of Ephraim and then of Dan followed after the precious vessels of the Sanctuary. Upon arrival at another site, the camp was pitched in its prescribed order, with the Tabernacle set up in readiness to receive the Holy Ark.

On two occasions, however, this order was changed. When Israel first departed from Mount Sinai, we read "the ark of the covenant of the LORD went before them in the three days' journey, to search out a resting place for them" (Num. 10.33). The other time we read of the Ark leading the children of Israel was when they crossed the river Jordan to go into the Promised Land.

Phoenician remains of an ivory carving of winged sphinxes with human faces, reminiscent of cherubim. "And there I will meet with thee, from above the mercy seat, from between the two cherubims which are upon the ark of the testimony, of all things which I will give thee in commandment unto the children of Israel" (Ex. 25.22).

The Wanderings in the Desert

The Wanderings of the Israelites in the Wilderness of Sinai

There is little consensus as to the route followed by the Israelites from Egypt to Sinai, but the trail of such sites as Wadi Gharandal, which can be identified with Elim and Wadi Feiran, where the events described as taking place in Rephidim could very possibly have occurred, leads to Ras Safsafeh. There is even less agreement as to how they proceeded from there to the Promised Land. Only the main stations of the journey recorded in the earlier part of the Book of Numbers can be identified with certainty — Hazeroth and Kadesh. Most of the sites mentioned in the detailed itinerary given in Numbers 33 are untraceable today as the names given to these sites by the Israelites often refer to events in which they were involved and thus would not be preserved in the names given them by the later Bedouin population. For example, the first "resting place" found for the Israelites by the Ark was subsequently called by God Taberah (from the Hebrew root, "to burn"), because of the fire that God spread among the people because of their complaining (Num. 11.1–3). The

Map showing the wanderings of the Israelites.

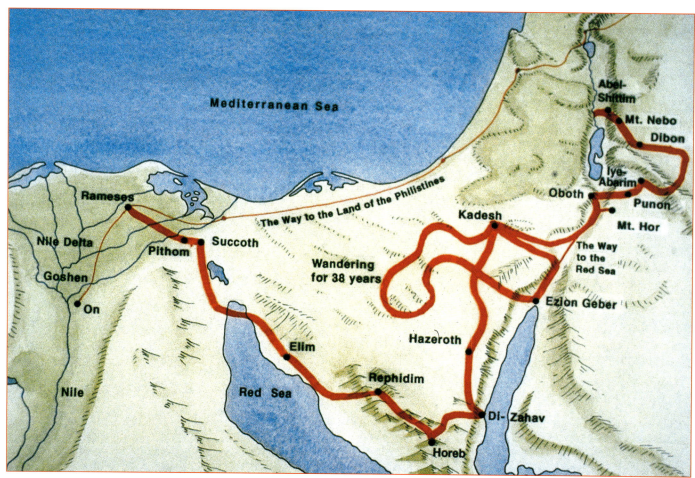

narrative does not say that they had moved to another site before another name, Kibroth-hattaavah (meaning "the graves of lust"), is given to it, after they gorge themselves on quails (Num. 11.34).

We are told that it was eleven days' journey from Horeb to Kadesh-barnea (Deut. 1.2). It would be a mistake, however, to assume that the Israelites went directly to Kadesh from Mount Sinai. They left the mountain where they had received God's laws in the second month of the second year (Num. 10.11) and appear to have taken almost a year to reach Kadesh (Deut. 2.14). This accords well with a detour over to the coast of the Gulf of Eilat touched on by a verse in Deuteronomy (1.1), which has Moses speaking to the children of Israel, "in the plain over against the Red sea, between Paran, and Tophel, and Laban, and Hazeroth, and Dizahab." Dizahab is almost universally identified with the present-day Dahab on the east coast of the Sinai Peninsula, about 47 miles or 75 km from Mount Sinai.

From there they would have journeyed inland to Hazeroth, which is today identified with Ein Hudra, a beautiful valley where they stayed for at least seven days, the period for which Miriam was shut out of the camp with leprosy (Num. 12.15). Their journey then brought them into the wilderness of Paran (the name apparently given to the desert of the Sinai peninsula), and the record in Numbers 13.26 leads to Kadesh-barnea. This is almost universally taken to be the site that is today known as Ein el-Qudeirat, a lush oasis with a copious spring in the northern Negeb. They had now reached the border of the Promised Land and Moses encouraged them, "Ye are come unto the mountain of the Amorites, which the Lord our God doth give unto us.

Behold, the Lord thy God hath set the land before thee: go up and possess it, as the Lord God of thy fathers hath said unto thee; fear not, neither be discouraged" (Deut. 1.20–21). From here the twelve spies, one for each tribe, were sent to report on conditions in the Land. Because of the lack of faith evident in their report and despite the encouragement of Joshua and Caleb, they were prevented from entering the Promised Land and left to wander in the desert for the next thirty-eight years.

Toward the end of their wanderings, it appears from the itinerary in Numbers 33 that the Israelites returned to Kadesh via Ezion-geber, present-day Eilat, at the northern end of the Gulf of Eilat. Moses requested permission from the King of Edom to go by way of the King's Highway but was refused. They then passed on to Mount Hor. Here Aaron the High Priest was buried. Numbers 33 details the route from Mount Hor to Zalmonah, Punon, Oboth, Iye-abarim on the border of Moab, Dibon-gad, Almon-diblathaim, and to the mountains of Abarim before Nebo, where Moses died in the plains of Moab by the Jordan near Jericho.

Additional information given in Numbers 21.4 shows that this must have meant returning to the Red Sea in order to avoid the Land of Edom. There is considerable dispute as to the accuracy of this itinerary with some scholars claiming that it does not reflect conditions in the area in the Late Bronze Age, around 1250 BC, the generally accepted date for the Exodus. However, contemporary lists found in Egypt contain many of the names mentioned in the latter part of the Numbers 33 listing. It thus appears that this was a well-known route linking the Arabah with the plains of Moab opposite Jericho.

Depiction of an Asiatic caravan, from wall painting in tomb of Khnum-hotep at Beni Hasan, c. 1890 BC.

Dizahab

Dizahab, an apparent detour from the traditional route of the Exodus, is mentioned as a place in which Moses spoke to all Israel. When the Holy Ark led the Israelites from Mount Sinai, they had spent a year camped before the mount and underwent a whole range of experiences — from terror when seeing the divine power in the quaking mountain, utter abandon in worshiping the Golden Calf, reverence of Moses for giving them God's commandments, to complete dedication in building the Tabernacle.

The Ark was to go "before them in the three days' journey, to search out a resting place for them" (Num. 10.33). What more restful place could it find than the plain alongside the loveliest and most delightful lagoon on the coast of the Gulf of Eilat?

We have a previous instance of God's loving foresight for the children of Israel when He "led them not through the way of the land of the Philistines, although that was near; for God said, Lest peradventure the people repent when they see war, and they return to Egypt"

View of Dahab, a lagoon on the eastern Sinai coast that has been identified as the site of Dizahab (meaning "golden"), mentioned in Deuteronomy 1.1.

but by a more circuitous route by way of the wilderness of the Red Sea (Ex. 13.17–18). This Dahab site is located some 47 miles or 75 km from Mount Sinai, which would be about three days' journey, if averaging 16 miles or 25 km a day.

In Numbers 11 there are two references to the sea. One is when the people crave for meat and Moses remarks: "Shall the flocks and the herds be slain for them, to suffice them? or shall all the fish of the sea be gathered together for them, to suffice them?" (v. 22). The other reference is when it is recorded that in fulfillment of God's promise that He would provide them with meat, "there went forth a wind from the Lord, and brought quails from the sea, and let them fall by the camp" (v. 31). Such mention of the sea is rare in the wilderness wanderings and could mean that the site of the encampment called Taberah and Kibroth-hattaavah was close to the seashore. The vivid marine colors and luxurious palm trees must have made a deep impression on those who emerged from the desert. But then, they would carry tragic memories from this place before leaving for Hazeroth—God's displeasure, the terrifying conflagration in the camp, and the plague from which many of their fellow Israelites had died.

Statuette of a bronze calf, symbol of fertility and strength, found in Ashkelon (2000-1550 BC).

Hazeroth

A desert oasis with palm trees.

Most explorers have identified Ein Hudra with the Hazeroth of the Bible, although the name simply means "enclosures" and the Hebrew root *hatzer* is to be found in many biblical place-names. However, as the (mostly) dry wadis or riverbeds were the highways of the desert, the path of the Israelites north to Kadesh-barnea, on the border of the Promised Land, would naturally lead them to this unique spring. To this day a cluster of palm trees marks its location, offering a welcome respite from the harsh desert.

The biblical narrative records that it was here in Hazeroth that Miriam was made leprous in punishment for her criticism of Moses' prominent position and of his marriage to an Ethiopian. The record says that she was shut out of the camp for seven days (Num. 12.15), so their sojourn here must have been at least for this length of time.

View of Wadi Hudra from the northeast, with the spring, Ein Hudra, visible in the distance at the end of the valley.

Kadesh-barnea

From the early twentieth century the valley of Ein el-Qudeirat has been identified as the site of Kadesh-barnea. Other oases in northern Sinai had been suggested in preference to this one. However, none of these have characteristics that point so compellingly in the direction of such an identification as does this one. Most importantly, this lush oasis is centered around the most copious spring in northern Sinai. It is also located at the intersection of two of the major desert routes: from Ezion-geber through the Arabah to Arad and Hebron in the north, and the Way of Shur from Egypt eastward to Edom. Another indication that this is the true location is found in the Scriptural references, Numbers 27.14 (among others) recording that it lay in the wilderness of Zin. This site indeed stands between two clearly defined geographical regions, with Sinai (or Paran) with its lofty grandeur in the southwest and the arid canyons and plateaus of the Negeb (or wilderness of Zin) to the northeast. It is also clear, from an early reference to Kadesh as En-mishpat (the Spring of Judgment) in Genesis 14.7 and other references to the site (Gen. 16.14, 20.1), that in the time of the Patriarchs the site was used as a place of gathering. This is evidenced by finds from that period that were excavated here.

The site was first surveyed by Leonard Woolley and T. E. Lawrence (Lawrence of Arabia) in 1914, just before the outbreak of the First World War. Excavations here were carried out by Moshe Dothan in 1956 and again by Rudolph Cohen between 1976 and 1982. The remains of three Israelite fortresses were uncovered, the earliest dating from the tenth or ninth century BC, the era of King Solomon. No

The valley of Ein el-Qudeirat, identified as the site of Kadesh-barnea. Toward the end of the valley are the remains of three Israelite fortresses.

traces of occupation from the Late Bronze Age (the period usually associated with the desert wanderings) were found. The excavations, however, were confined to a restricted area and evidence of the Israelites' stay at Kadesh-barnea is yet to be discovered.

It is not known how long they stayed in Kadesh-barnea, but it was for at least forty days while they waited for the spies to return from their survey of the Land (Num. 13.25). The record in Deuteronomy 1.46 gives the impression that they remained there for a considerable length of time: "So ye abode in Kadesh many days, according unto the days that ye abode there." Apart from the dispatch of the spies and their dramatic return, a number of pivotal events on the way to the Promised Land, such as Korah's rebellion, the budding of Aaron's rod, Moses' smiting of the rock and the death of Miriam, all took place in Kadesh. Some thirty-eight years of wandering intervened between the first and last two incidents.

The site was called Meribah Kadesh (the "Strife" of Kadesh) when Moses hit the rock twice in order to provide the Israelites with water instead of speaking to the rock as he had been commanded to do (Num. 20.1–13). Kadesh-barnea later appears in the delineation of the southern border of Judah (Josh. 15.3).

Today, the valley is farmed extensively by local Bedouin, who grow fruit, vegetables and olives. In some parts of the valley there are dams to trap water from the powerful spring.

Plan of the middle fortress, eighth–seventh centuries BC.

Nineteenth century engraving of the Spring of Moses.

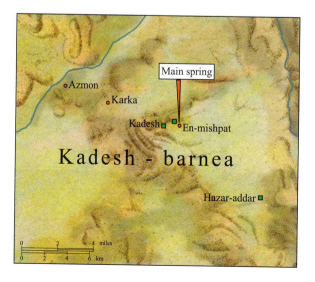

Kadesh-barnea. "So ye abode in Kadesh many days, according unto the days that ye abode there" (Deut. 1.46).

Facing the Promised Land

The Encampment of the Israelites in the Plains of Moab

The next station of which the Bible presents a vivid picture is the encampment in the plains of Moab by the River Jordan near Jericho. Here, after the circuitous journey of the Israelites around Edom, their decisive victory over Sihon the king of the Amorites, and defeat of Og the king of Bashan, they pitched their tents for the last time outside the land that had been promised them. The location of their final encampment east of the Jordan River is so minutely described in Scripture that we can almost see the lines of tents standing around the Tabernacle in this lush corner of the river valley.

It is the last of the forty-five stations enumerated in Numbers 33. Here it is recorded, "And they departed from the mountains of Abarim, and pitched in the plains of Moab by Jordan near Jericho. And they pitched by Jordan, from Beth-jesimoth even unto Abel-shittim in the plains of Moab" (v. 48–49).

Whereas in the northern part of the Jordan valley the plain is no more than 8 miles (13 km) wide, it widens to 14 miles at its southern end where it flows into the Dead Sea. Here the waters that flow along Wadi Kelt combine with other springs to create the green oasis of Jericho, while across the Jordan a corresponding patch of verdure is formed by the springs that issue from the lower foothills of Moab. The sites of Abel-shittim and Beth-jesimoth have been located here at either end of this well-irrigated stretch of plain bordering the east bank of the Jordan.

Josephus Flavius, the first-century historian, describes Abel-shittim, which in his day was known as Abila, as "a region thickly planted with palm trees" (*Jewish Antiquities* 4.176). The southerly position of Beth-jesimoth can be deduced from its place in the enumeration of the towns of Reuben in Joshua 13.20. In the time of Christ, the Roman city of Livias (Julias) stood here. Some rabbinical sources estimate the Israelite encampment as being 12 miles or 19 km long (*Lev. R.* 20, 52b, p. *Sheb.* 36e, b. *Yoma* 75b).

This dramatic view of the Israelites poised for the long-awaited entry to the Promised Land formed part of the panorama seen first by Balaam and shortly afterwards by Moses from the lofty mountaintops above. Balaam, the Mesopotamian prophet hired by Balak the king of Moab to curse the Israelites, saw their camp from three positions.

From the first, Bamoth Baal (the high places of Baal), he had a limited view and could see only "the utmost part of the people" (Num. 22.41). The second station was the field of Zophim (the gazers) or the top of Pisgah (the hill). This Pisgah is the highest point in the ridge that juts out from the plateau of the mountains of Moab, just opposite the northern end of the Dead Sea. However despite its height, about 2,625 feet (800 m), the view is hampered by the surrounding hills (Num. 23.13). It was only when Balak brought Balaam to the lower summit, known in Scripture as "the top of Peor, that looketh toward Jeshimon" (Num. 23.28) and at present Siyagha, that an unimpeded

The first-century historian Josephus Flavius, as pictured in a nineteenth-century book illustration.

A bronze figurine (c. 1550–1200 BC) of Baal, the Canaanite god who was worshiped on high places in Moab in the time of Balaam and Balak (Num. 22.41).

The Israelite encampment in the plains of Moab opposite Jericho. In this drawing, the scene is set for the entry of the Israelites into the Promised Land. The site of Adam, where the waters of the river stood up in a heap allowing the Israelites to cross the Jordan, is indicated.

view of the Israelite camp opened before him. Thus he was inspired to declaim, "How goodly are thy tents, O Jacob, and thy tabernacles, O Israel!" (Num. 24.5) and in spite of his malevolent intentions, he did bless Israel.

Balaam concludes his parable with a view of Edom to the south, Amalek toward the southwest and the Kenites just opposite over the Dead Sea. He then turns his thoughts to Asshur, his own land far to the north, and prophesies that ships from Chittim would come to trouble her.

Moses ascended to another vantage point when God commanded him, "Get thee up into the top of Pisgah and lift up thine eyes westward, and northward, and southward, and eastward, and behold it with thine eyes: for thou shalt not go over this Jordan" (Deut. 3.27). The mountain may have been called after the pagan god Nebo (Deut. 34.1) but Balaam's "top of Peor, that looketh toward Jeshimon" the wilderness (Num. 23.28) and Moses' "Pisgah, that is over against Jericho" must be one and the same. However the views they saw were quite different. After surveying the encampment of the Israelites and

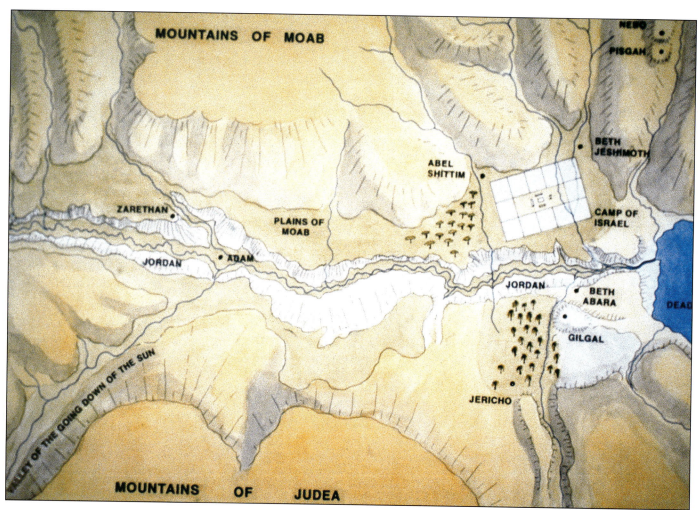

The mountains of Moab from En-gedi, nineteenth century engraving.

prophesying about them, Balaam looked in every direction but knew only the political settlement pattern of the time when pagan tribes possessed the Land.

Moses' view, on the other hand, was imbued with faith and he envisioned the future inheritance of his people, although he himself was not allowed to enter the Promised Land. The tribal portions had not yet been allocated but Scripture records that as he turned his head, God showed him the hills of Gilead with their oak woods that were to be given to Gad and to the half-tribe of Manasseh in the north. To the northwest lay the gentle hills of Naphtali. The land of Ephraim and the other portion of Manasseh were visible in the west. The hill country of Judah loomed in the southwest with the Negeb desert to the far south. Although Dan did not receive its additional portion in the north of the land, near the source of Jordan, until over a hundred years later, it is already mentioned. This view of the Promised Land and the camp of the Israelites waiting to enter it was the last thing Moses saw. He was buried by an angel in a valley below the plateau of Nebo. The exact place of his burial is unknown.

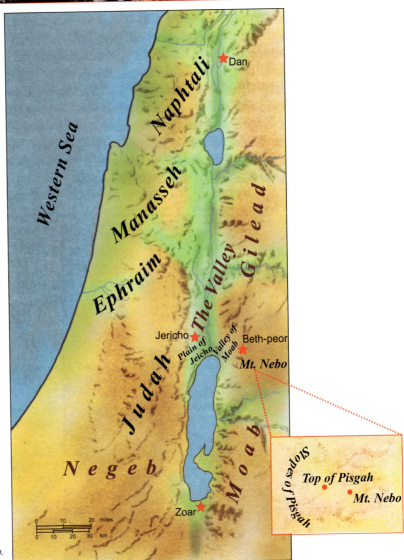

View of the Promised Land from Mount Nebo.

23

Crossing the River Jordan

Although Moses could not lead his people into the Promised Land and had appointed Joshua as his successor, his commitments, as recorded in Scripture, were honored to the last. In fact, the whole event, possibly the most momentous for the Israelites since the crossing of the Red Sea, is summed up: "everything was finished that the Lord commanded Joshua to speak unto the people, according to all that Moses commanded Joshua" (Josh. 4.10).

Before the crossing, Joshua sent the two spies to gather intelligence on Jericho, the key to the conquest of the Promised Land. About the same time, the encampment moved from Abel-shittim to the banks of the Jordan itself. There they were told that within three days, they were to cross the river to receive their inheritance.

It must have been a test of faith even to approach the river at harvest time when the river overflowed its banks (Josh. 3.15). Specifically, it was the time of barley harvest, as the references to the first month and to the fact that the Passover was observed four days after the crossing make clear (Josh. 5.10). At that time the snows of Mount Hermon melt and the sudden volume of water turn the shallow stream into a swiftly flowing river with

A rare photograph from the nineteenth century showing the River Jordan overflowing its banks in the springtime.

treacherous currents. Such an obstacle was no deterrent to the two spies on their way to and from Jericho. They would have been chosen on the basis of their strength as well as their reliability. However, for the majority of the Israelites it would have impossible to cross the Jordan at that time of year, as the fords that were normally used were impassable.

The Jordan River has two terraces, the upper one known as *kikar ha-yarden* (the plain of Jordan) and the lower, where the river still meanders today, called *gaon ha-yarden* (the pride or swelling of the Jordan). Because of periodic flooding, the lowest level was hot and humid, encouraging the growth of a dense thicket of sycamore, willow and other trees and bushes. During flooding, the wild animals that inhabited this jungle-like vegetation would flee the lower terrace for higher ground. Even today, the lower valley supports a population of foxes, hyenas, wild boars and wolves. The English expedition that sailed down the Jordan in the nineteenth century estimated the Jordan in flood to be half a mile wide.

In this part of the story, the Ark of the Covenant again comes to the fore. Not since the Israelites had left Mount Sinai/Horeb on a three-day journey had the Ark gone before them but had been kept in place at the center of the tribal groupings. Here, after the three days' preparation on the banks of the Jordan, the officers commanded the people, "When ye see the ark of the covenant of the Lord your God, and the priests the Levites bearing it, then ye shall remove from your place, and go after it. Yet there shall be a space between you and it, about two thousand cubits by measure: come not near unto it, that ye may know the way by which ye must go: for ye have not passed this way heretofore" (Josh. 3.3–4).

The distance of two thousand cubits (0.65 mile or 1 km) ensured that it could be clearly seen. As soon as the feet of the priests that carried the Ark touched the waters of the Jordan, the river "stood and rose up upon a heap very far from [Hebrew, in] the city Adam that is beside Zaretan" (Josh. 3.16). Zaretan must have been a well-known landmark and Tell es-Saidiyeh, an imposing mound in the center of the Rift Valley, has been tentatively proposed as the site of this biblical city. Adam has been identified with Tell Damiya, some 18 miles or 30 km from the place of the Israelite

crossing opposite Jericho and the site of the present-day Adam Bridge. If this identification is correct, the Israelites had quite a long stretch of dry riverbed over which they could cross in safety. As it is recorded that they "hasted and passed over," apparently in one day, large numbers of people must have crossed at the same time, perhaps making use of the entire length of dry riverbed.

While the priests stood with the Ark in the Jordan, the Reubenites, Gadites and the half-tribe of Manasseh, fully armed, led the other

Crossing the River Jordan.

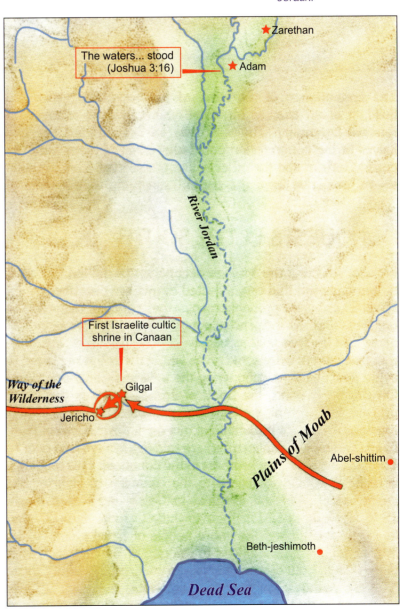

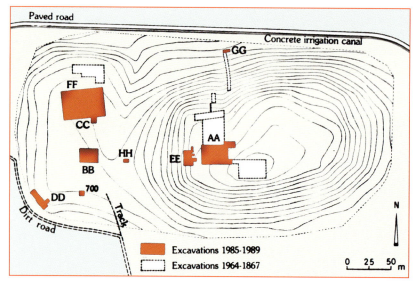

GG

FF

CC

AA

HH

EE

BB

DD   700

Dirt road

Track

N

Excavations 1985-1989

Excavations 1964-1867

0   25   50 m

Plan of Tell es-Saidiyeh and view of the excavation areas.

tribes across the river realizing the promise made to them by Moses. Two memorials of twelve stones taken from the river were set up, one in the middle of Jordan and another at Gilgal, their first encampment in the Land of Promise. Here they celebrated the Passover. In modern times, the river Jordan has been blocked on a number of occasions by landslides and mud caused by earthquakes. In 1267, a large mound slid into the river near Damiya blocking its flow for sixteen hours. In the earthquake of 1927, a mudslide cut off the river, also near Damiya, this time for twenty-four hours.

Ancient Jericho

In biblical times, Jericho was renowned for its luxuriant palm trees, so much so that the names Jericho and "city of palm trees" (Deut. 34.3, etc.) were interchangeable. In the Roman period, Josephus, Pliny and others write of the magnificence of Jericho's palm trees. Indeed, its palm groves and precious gardens of balsam were numbered among the gifts given by Antony to Cleopatra of Egypt.

In the time of Joshua, the formidable city walls of Jericho loomed high above these trees. The city's inhabitants would have observed the events of the previous weeks: the move from Abel-shittim, the miraculous and what must have been to them terrifying crossing of the Jordan, and the setting up of the camp in Gilgal, where silence would have reigned after the entire male population apart from Joshua and Caleb were circumcised before the observance of the Passover. Joshua must have been made aware of the morale of the people within the walls by the reports of the spies. Rahab the harlot, who had hidden the two spies, confessed "our hearts did melt, neither did there remain any more courage in any man, because of you: for the Lord your God, he is God in heaven above, and in earth beneath" (Josh. 2.11).

Here again in the capture of Jericho, the Ark of the Covenant is the focal point. The people of Jericho would have wondered at what followed. Obeying God's commands to Joshua, the Israelites marched around the city once, the armed men preceding seven priests blowing trumpets who went before the Ark that was borne aloft by its staves. The multitudes of Israelites followed behind what apparently was a very impressive procession, particularly because it was carried out in complete silence apart from the sound of the trumpets. This same ritual was conducted on six successive days.

On the seventh day, however, the procession made its relentless circuit, not once, but seven times. At a pre-arranged signal — a long blast from the trumpets — all the Israelites raised a "great shout" at which the wall of the city collapsed. In fulfillment of the promise made to Rahab, her house, which stood on the town walls, was spared and she and her family were taken out of the city to the camp of Israel. All that was in the city and its inhabitants were set on fire, apart from the vessels of silver and gold and other metals which were put into the treasury.

The battle was won but archaeologists have long been at war over the interpretation of these events in light of the material remains. Tell es-Sultan (ancient Jericho) was first excavated by an Austro-German team under the direction of Ernst Sellin and Carl Watzinger in the first decade of the twentieth century. They concluded that the site was unoccupied during the Late Bronze Age (1550–1200 BC), the period in which the Israelites are thought to have entered the Land. The American archaeologist John Garstang disagreed with their conclusion and his expedition (1929–1936) found evidence here of the destruction of a city in about 1400 BC, which he attributed to the Israelites. The British archaeologist, Dame Kathleen Kenyon, who excavated here from 1952 to 1958, denied that there was any evidence of an Israelite conquest in Jericho. She deduced from the absence of a particular type of Late Bronze pottery that there had been no conquest. Although her work was meticulous and well documented, her conclusions put the dating of the Exodus in question. Recently, pro-Bible scholars such as American Bryant Wood, who carried out an analysis of the Jericho pottery, and Englishman John Bimson, have suggested placing the Exodus in the fifteenth century BC, when the archaeological remains and the biblical record are in harmony.

Excavations in Jericho revealed a stone revetment wall, some 15 feet (4.50 m) high, which surrounded the ancient city, with a mudbrick parapet on top. This wall formed the city's outer line of defense. Inside this line was a sloping earthen rampart on which houses were built as was the city's inner defense wall, also of mudbrick. The houses in the city proper were of superior construction. Clear evidence of destruction has been found in which both the

"And it came to pass, when Joshua had spoken unto the people, that the seven priests bearing the seven trumpets of rams' horns passed on before the Lord, and blew with the trumpets" (Josh. 6.8).

Clay human head (8300-5500 BC) found in ancient Jericho.

stone revetment wall and the mudbrick parapet wall collapsed. Houses on the plastered rampart were also demolished and the piles of collapsed bricks lie against the base of the revetment wall. This last detail is in accord with the description of the Israelites' entry: "the people went up into the city, every man straight before him, and they took the city" (Josh. 6.20).

There is also evidence of a conflagration of the entire city of this period. Apart from the ubiquitous pottery, large quantities of grain were found in the storage areas of the houses such as one would expect just after harvest. Usually, city conquerors would take the precious grain stores for themselves. However, the Israelites were under a "herem" or ban (Josh. 6.17), whereby they were forbidden to take away any spoils from the captured city. There is a clear correlation between this destruction level of ancient Jericho and the Israelite conquest, but revisions in the traditional chronology are necessary if the archaeological evidence and the Bible record are to be brought into accord.

View of ancient Jericho, looking in a southeasterly direction through the palm trees at the mound of ancient Jericho. The modern town of Jericho lies beyond the tell. Gilgal, where the practice of circumcision was reinstituted, lay somewhere on rising ground (Josh. 5.3) between Jericho and the Jordan River to the east beyond the belt of green. There is an interesting reference to the memorial set up in Gilgal by the Israelites in Judges 3.19, when Ehud goes on his mission to kill Eglon, the king of Moab, who was oppressing Israel at that time. The record refers to Ehud turning again "from the quarries [Hebrew, sculptures] that were by Gilgal."

Plan of Tell es-Sultan (ancient Jericho) and the excavation areas.

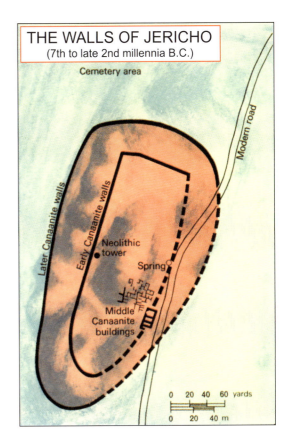

THE WALLS OF JERICHO
(7th to late 2nd millennia B.C.)

Cemetery area

Modern road

Later Canaanite walls

Early Canaanite walls

Neolithic tower

Spring

Middle Canaanite buildings

| 0 | 20 | 40 | 60 yards |

| 0 | 20 | 40 m |

The Sultan's Spring (Ein es Sultan), commonly called the Fountain of Elisha, in the plain of Jericho, nineteenth century engraving.

Entering the Promised Land

The Valley "Where the Sun Goeth Down"

View from the north of Wadi Fari'a or the "Valley Where the Sun Goeth Down" which the Israelites traversed to reach the mountains of Ebal and Gerizim, where Moses had commanded them to pronounce the blessing and the cursing.

The valley "where the sun goeth down" (Hebrew, *derech mevo ha-shemesh*) is the way which Moses had commanded the Israelites to go to reach the mountains of Ebal and Gerizim. "And it shall come to pass, when the Lord thy God hath brought thee in unto the land whither thou goest to possess it, that thou shalt put the blessing upon mount Gerizim, and the curse upon mount Ebal. Are they not on the other side Jordan, by *the way where the sun goeth down*, in the land of the Canaanites, which dwell in the champaign over against Gilgal, beside the plains of Moreh?" (Deut. 11.29–30).

It is significant that this command was fulfilled within a few days of the Israelites' entry to the Promised Land. Apparently Gilgal, the site of their first encampment on this side of the Jordan, became their first permanent settlement. Here, beside the luxuriant palm grove and the waters of Wadi Kelt, the generation born in the wilderness could settle down for the first time in their lives. The fighting men, however, could not rest. The ruins of Jericho were probably still smoldering when the next city, Ai, was taken.

Despite their confidence, the men of Ai being "but few" (Josh. 7.3), the Israelites were initially defeated. Here we are reminded again of the centrality of the Holy Ark in the life of the Israelites. Joshua and the elders of Israel fell before the Ark to entreat God's help. An Israelite had taken something from Jericho, the city that was accursed, and the ceremony of the Tabernacle was the means God used to find out who was guilty. The method of discernment probably involved the breastplate of the High Priest with its Urim (lights) and Thummim (perfections). How exactly it worked is unclear. Once the culprit was discovered and punished, they returned to Ai, this time to victory.

They were not to rest on their laurels, however. Joshua's first deed after taking Ai was to fulfill Moses' command: "Then Joshua built an altar unto the Lord God of Israel in mount Ebal" (Josh. 8.30). Here it was not just the fighting men who were involved — the record in Joshua emphasizes that "all Israel" were part of this great assembly. The entire nation left their newfound home in Gilgal to trek up this valley into the heart of enemy territory when they had so far conquered only two cities. This time the Ark went alone, without the Tabernacle.

Today, the valley is called Wadi Fari'a. It is still the major east-west route in this part of the Samarian mountain range. It runs from the Jordan Valley near the Adam Bridge up to just north of Nablus, ancient Shechem. In summer, when the sun sets, its rays fill the valley. The traveler coming up from the Jordan would see the sun set exactly at the end of the valley.

An artist's depiction of the High Priest's breastplate.

Mount Ebal and Mount Gerizim

George Adam Smith, whose incomparable Historical Geography of the Holy Land, *written toward the end of the nineteenth century, is still a handbook for those interested in the character of the Land, wrote: "Towards the end of the range (the central range of*

The place where the blessing and the cursing were to be pronounced was well chosen. Apart from its centrality, the area of Mount Ebal and Mount Gerizim had strong patriarchal associations. Here Abraham built his first altar in the Land (Gen. 12.6–7). Jacob not only built the altar which he called El-elohe-Israel here but he also bought land in Shechem (Gen. 33.18–20). It thus seems probable that it was at this time, in the first days of their entrance to the Land, that the tribes of Ephraim and Manasseh fulfilled the oath taken of them by Joseph to bring up his bones from Egypt to rest in the Land of Israel (Gen. 50.24–26). They must have had this very place in mind during the many years they carried the embalmed body of Joseph on their wanderings. The record in Acts 7.16 records the conclusion of their burden-bearing: "And they (the bones of Joseph) were carried over into Sychem and laid in the sepulchre that Abraham bought for a sum of money of the sons of Emmor the father of Sychem."

Since its departure from Sinai, we have encountered scenes of powerful drama in which the Holy Ark has played a central role. Few of these scenes nor indeed of those yet to come could rank in dignity with the pronouncement of the blessing and the cursing here against this singular backdrop.

Picture the scene — firstly, the people had to witness the erection on Mount Ebal of two structures, the pattern of which had been laid down by Moses before his death. The altar had to be of complete, unworked stones (Deut. 27.5–6), in conformity also with the general laws concerning altars given in Exodus (20.25). The second structure was unprecedented — it consisted of an unspecified number of great stones set upright on which the law (or parts of it) was written on a specially prepared surface (Deut. 27.2–4). For the Israelites, the sight of this written portrayal of the words they had heard from the mouth of Moses in this surpassingly beautiful spot must have been

mountains) two bold round hills break the sky-line, with evidence of a deep valley between them. The hills are Ebal and Gerizim and in the valley, the only real pass across the range, lies Nablus, anciently Shechem. That the eye is thus drawn from the first upon the position of Shechem ... while all the other chief sites of Israel's life lie hidden and are scarcely to be seen till you come upon them is a remarkable fact which we emphasize in passing."

Smith calls this area the "obvious centre" of the land and goes on to write, "Of the two hills beside Shechem, Gerizim is the more famous historically, but Ebal is higher and has the further prospect. The view from Ebal virtually covers the whole land, with the exception of the Negeb. All the four long zones, two of the four frontiers, specimens of all the physical features and most of the famous scenes of the history, are in sight. No geography of Palestine can afford to dispense with the view from the top of Ebal" (The Historical Geography of the Holy Land, 25th ed., London, Hodder and Stoughton, 1931, Reprint ed., London, Fontana, 1966, p.4).

Map of Mount Gerizim and Mount Ebal.

Mt. Gerizim

Mt. Ebal

Shechem

awesome. Sacrifices of burnt offerings and peace offerings were made on the altar and then came the main focus of the assembly.

Over on Mount Gerizim stood the tribes of Simeon, Levi, Judah, Issachar, Joseph and Benjamin ready to do the blessing. Prepared to curse were Reuben, Gad, Asher, Zebulun, Dan and Naphtali on Mount Ebal. In the valley between them was the Ark borne by the priests. The cursing was first pronounced and the

congregation's Amen must have resounded long after the people had pronounced it given the amazing acoustics of the place. Then followed the blessing, also answered by a series of loud Amens. The Israelites were left with the stark choice offered to them by Moses (Deut. 30.19): "I call heaven and earth to record this day against you, that I have set before you life and death, blessing and cursing: therefore choose life, that both thou and thy seed may live."

A structure discovered in 1982 by archaeologist Adam Zertal on the northeastern slope of Mount Ebal was initially identified as Joshua's altar. Other archaeologists however were not convinced. In any case, although the view from this site is spectacular, the location of this structure is out of view of anyone standing in the valley between Ebal and Gerizim.

Small, limestone four-horned altar from the Iron Age, found at Megiddo. "And if thou wilt make me an altar of stone, thou shalt not build it of hewn stone" (Ex. 20.25).

Shiloh

During the long wars waged by the Israelites against the Canaanites in the heartland of the country, the Tabernacle and the Ark stayed in Gilgal. Then, in Joshua 18.1, we read, "And the whole congregation assembled together at Shiloh, and set up the tabernacle of the congregation there." In contrast to many of the sites we have encountered, Shiloh is devoid of any notable features. Today all that remains is a small, secluded tell of not more than 8 acres, at the end of a fertile and peaceful valley in the heart of the hill country of Ephraim.

However, despite the unremarkable siting, Shiloh is the most meticulously defined place in the whole of Scripture. At the end of the book of Judges (21.19), we read "Behold, there is a feast of the Lord in Shiloh yearly in a place which is on the north side of Beth-el, on the east side of the highway that goeth up from Beth-el to Shechem, and on the south of Lebonah." The Authorized Version obscures the accuracy of this description by adding "in a place" where it does not exist in the original Hebrew. The Scriptural description is of the precise location of Shiloh itself. Since the days of Robinson, who in the 1830s identified many biblical place names, the Arab village of Beitin some 10 miles (16 km) north of Jerusalem has been identified with Bethel. The ancient highway from Bethel to Shechem followed a similar route to its modern counterpart and Lebonah is universally identified with the Arab village of Lubban. Despite the precision of the biblical description, the vastly more dramatic site of Nebi Samwil on the outskirts of Jerusalem was frequently taken as Shiloh. Authorities such as Jerome and Eusebius in the fourth century had correctly identified the tell of Seilun with Shiloh as did a few medieval scholars, but it was again Dr. Robinson who brought the correct identification to light.

It was probably the very seclusion that determined its choice as the new site of the Tabernacle. Here the tribal allotment of territory could proceed unhampered by interference by the Canaanites, who still held

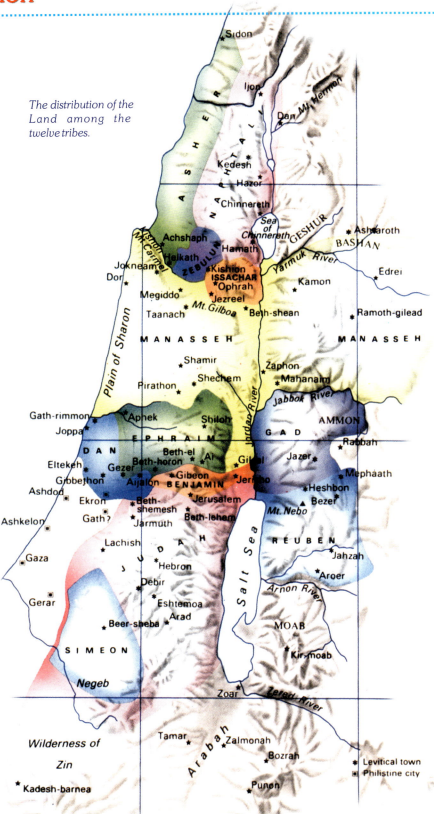

The distribution of the Land among the twelve tribes.

large areas farther to the north and south. Its central location too facilitated the task in hand. Already at Gilgal the tribes of Judah, Ephraim and the remaining half-tribe of Manasseh had received their portions (Josh. 14–17). From Shiloh, three men of each of the remaining seven tribes were sent out to measure the land. After the details had been recorded, these tribes too received their inheritance. Scripture records that the allotment of the portions was determined by the casting of lots (Josh. 18.10), thus again the Urim and the Thummim of the High Priest may have been involved. We can be certain that the allotment was carried out "at the door of the tabernacle of the congregation" (Josh. 19.51), emphasizing the centrality of the Tabernacle in all the actions of the people. This process, which must have taken a considerable amount of time, was followed by the appointment of six cities of refuge and the provision of cities for the Levites among the other tribes (Josh. 20.21).

Shiloh later became the permanent seat of the priesthood. The story of Hannah and Samuel in the first chapters of the book of Samuel takes place against the background of Eli as High Priest. From these chapters, we get the impression that the Tabernacle was in some sort of permanent structure referred to as the "house of the Lord" (Hebrew, *beth Yahweh*) (1 Sam. 1.7, 1.24, etc.), in contrast to the movable structure which was continually erected and dismantled during the wanderings in the wilderness. The Mishnah says as much: "After they came to Shiloh, the high places were forbidden. There was no roof-beam there, but below was a house of stone and above were hangings and this was the 'resting place'" (*Zebachim* 14.6).

The tell of Seilun was first excavated by two Danish expeditions in the 1920s and 1930s. Although their excavations were confined to a limited area, they were able to determine that the town had been destroyed by the Philistines in the mid-eleventh century BC. An Israeli expedition, led by I. Finkelstein, S. Bunimovitz and Z. Ledermann, excavated the tell between 1981 and 1984 as part of the survey of the Land of Ephraim. The Romans and Byzantines had built on the summit of the mound and destroyed any earlier remains in their efforts to get down to bedrock. Thus the team of

An isometric reconstruction of two Iron Age or Early Israelite buildings built into and against a Middle Bronze Age city wall at Shiloh. These pillared buildings contained an abundance of early Israelite pottery with over twenty of the collar-rim jars that characterize Israelite settlement in this part of the Land.

archaeologists concentrated on the edges of the mound which had no later construction. From the biblical point of view, the most interesting finds were made in their Area C, which had been partially explored by the Danish expedition and which lay on the west of the tell.

Here two Iron Age or Early Israelite buildings built into and against a Middle Bronze Age city wall were uncovered. Evidence shows destruction by fire. Because of the ritual nature of objects found in the debris above the destruction level, it was suggested that these buildings stood at the back end of a large structure of a cultic nature on the summit. Can we deduce from this that the Tabernacle stood on the summit? Certainty is impossible in view of the destruction of the earlier remains in this area.

However, the tell of Seilun is undoubtedly the ancient Shiloh and the pillared buildings are authentic remains from the stirring times which saw the erection of the Tabernacle in its new home in the mountains of Ephraim.

Map of the mound of Shiloh, its excavated areas and plan of the principal remains.

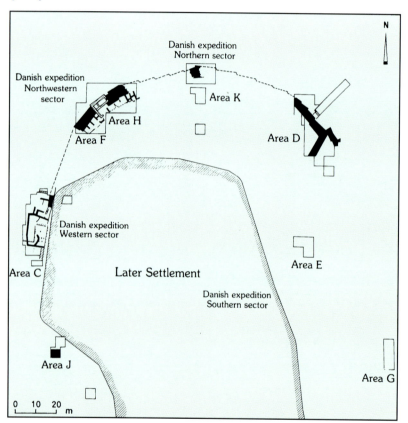

Ancient gateway at Shiloh, nineteenth century engraving.

Charles Wilson

An alternative suggestion for the location of the Tabernacle was made by Capt. Charles Wilson. A Royal Engineer, he carried out surveys in many parts of the country in the 1870s, also visiting the tell of Seilun. He believed that a large open stone court on the north of the mound was a likely location for the ritual center of Shiloh. However, recent excavations of very limited extent by Zeev Yeivin failed to discover any Iron Age remains in this area.

From Philistine Captivity to Kiriath-jearim

Aphek

Aphek, where the Philistines assembled for their notable battle with the Israelites, was the place where the drama began which sent the Holy Ark on seven months of wandering through enemy territory until the damage it inflicted was so great that it was sent away. The next episode in its history saw it secluded on a hilltop near Jerusalem guarded by Gentiles for twenty years and then in the home of a man from Philistine Gath, until King David put it into the tent which he pitched for it in his newly found capital.

The site of Aphek marked the northern border of the Philistines and was very strong strategically. It guarded the road from the coastal plain to the hill country where the Israelites had settled. The battle waged here was one of many in the constant struggle between the Israelites and the Philistines over control of the country's key routes. Aphek lies near the source of the river Yarkon that flows into the Mediterranean Sea near Tel Aviv.

The exact location of Eben-ezer, where the Israelites assembled for battle, is unclear but it is thought to have been east of Aphek on the edge of the Judean foothills. A site known as Izbet Sartah perched on one of these hills overlooking Aphek has been identified as the rallying place of the Israelites. Defeat seemed unavoidable. When four thousand Israelites fell on the first day, the elders sent for the Ark of the Covenant in Shiloh to help lead them in battle. Although terror had seized the army of the Philistines they were still victorious, completely routing the Israelites. The news

that the battle had been lost and the Ark taken into captivity brought Eli to his death (1 Sam. 4). Although it is not recorded in the biblical narrative, it would appear from other references in the Scripture that the Philistines then proceeded to destroy Shiloh. The prophet Jeremiah recalls the destruction of Shiloh to warn the people of his time to mend their ways: "But go ye now unto my place which was in Shiloh, where I set my name at the first, and see what I did to it for the wickedness of my people Israel" (Jer. 7.12).

Inside and adjacent to the Turkish citadel, the site of Aphek shows an extensive range of occupation with levels from the Early Bronze Age through to the Turkish. It was surveyed by W. F. Albright in 1923 and excavated under the

The battle of Eben-ezer.

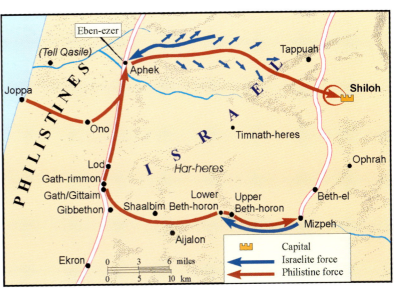

Map of the mound of Aphek, its excavation areas and general plan of the principal remains.

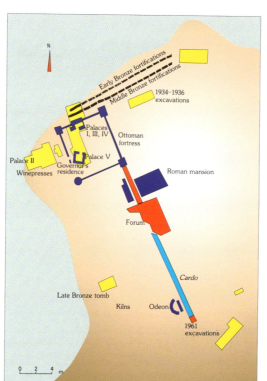

direction of A. Eitan in 1961. The site was again excavated by M. Kochavi and P. Beck from 1972 to 1985. Two strata are characterized by large quantities of Philistine pottery but the finds seem to indicate that it was merely a stronghold and not a large occupied center.

A view toward the east of the Turkish fortress that today stands on the site of Aphek where the Philistines assembled for their first notable battle with the Israelites. It lies about 10 miles or 16 km inland and northeast of Tel Aviv on the road from Jerusalem to Caesarea. The site is better known by the name Antipatris, given to it by Herod who built there a memorial to his father. Josephus records that "he founded a city in the fairest plain in his realm, rich in rivers and trees and named it Antipatris" (War 1.417). Today the tell lies within the confines of a large park offering a pleasant respite from the bustle of nearby Tel Aviv.

The Philistines

While the newly arrived Israelites were establishing their settlements in the hill country with Shiloh as their civic center, the Philistines, also newly arrived from the Aegean, were settling on the coastal plain. That the Philistines were part of a massive movement of people called the Sea Peoples that occurred in the eastern Mediterranean at the end of the thirteenth century BC is clear. What is unclear is precisely what brought about this upheaval which resulted in the destruction of the great Mycenean palaces in Greece, the crumbling of the Hittite empire in the area of Turkey, and the destruction of Ugarit in what is today Syria. Egypt was one of the few civilizations not totally destabilized. Whatever caused this disintegration and natural disaster, such as famine, drought or earthquake, is now believed to be more likely than the regional hostilities previously considered to be the cause, it resulted in the invasion of Canaan by a number of warlike tribes, whose archaeological record is vastly different to that of the Israelites.

The Bible tells us the precise areas in which the Philistines lived. In 1 Samuel, their confederation of five cities on the coastal plain — Ashdod, Gaza, Ashkelon, Gath and Ekron — are listed. The first three of these cities have kept their original names while Ekron has been identified with Tel Miqne, which lies 22 miles (35 km) southwest of Jerusalem on the western edge of the coastal plain, and Gath with Tell es-Safi nearby. Of these sites, Ashdod, Ashkelon and Gath have been excavated and the distinctiveness of the finds from the twelfth century BC that were found there from those of the Israelite settlement in the hill country is very

The head of a typical Philistine warrior as portrayed in a stone carving on the walls of Medinet Habu, the mortuary temple of Pharaoh Rameses III in Thebes, Egypt. This head is a small detail of two large scenes which portray two great battles of the Egyptians against the Philistines. The feathered headdress of the Sea Peoples makes them clearly distinguishable from the other figures depicted in these reliefs. When we see the cruelty evident in such faces and realize that it was into the hands of such people that the Ark of the Covenant was now delivered, the words of the psalm, "he forsook the tabernacle of Shiloh, the tent he placed among men. And delivered his strength into captivity and his glory into the enemy's hand" (Ps. 78.60–61), come home with full force.

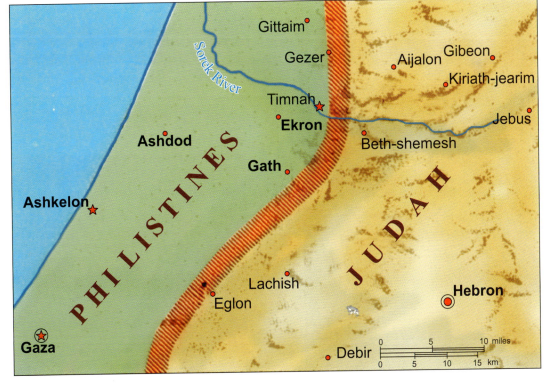

The land of the Philistines.

striking. Clearly this was a new element in the country with a vibrant material culture. Their characteristic pottery is reminiscent of sophisticated Aegean prototypes, but scientific analysis shows that it was made of local clay. Additional evidence of their Aegean origin is to be found in the architectural style of the large urban centers they constructed on the ruins of much smaller Canaanite cities. Central hearths such as were common in the palaces of Mycene have been found at Ekron and Tel Qasile, another Philistine site near present-day Tel Aviv. The excavation record also confirms what the Bible tells us about the Philistines having a monopoly on ironworking and of the Israelites having to go down from the hill country to the coastal plain to procure iron implements (1 Sam. 13.19–21). Very few iron tools have been found from this period in the hill country, bronze being the metal in common usage. In the Philistine context however, although the use of iron does not become widespread until the ninth century BC, the quality of their metalwork is unquestioned.

Their language is unknown, as no Philistine inscriptions have yet been discovered. Definite ideas as to their appearance, however, can be derived from the most important records we have of these Sea Peoples, the reliefs and inscriptions from Medinet Habu.

1. War of Rameses III against the Sea Peoples, from relief of Rameses III at Medinet Habu.

2. Siege of city in Land of Amurru, from relief of Rameses III at Medinet Habu.

1.

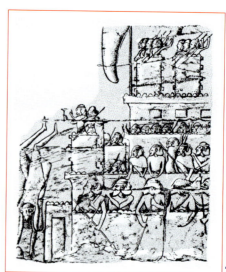

2.

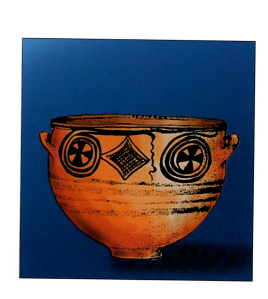

Decorated Philistine bowl and jug, twelfth to eleventh centuries BC.

The Wanderings of the Ark among the Philistines

The Scriptural record of the wanderings of the Ark among the Philistines provides a vivid picture of the Philistine region in the coastal plain. Its fertility and proximity to the sea must have attracted these seafarers to this low-lying area. However, of all the five Philistine cities, Ashkelon is the only one situated on the seashore. The Ark was first taken to Ashdod, a large, heavily fortified city about 3 miles (5 km) south of the present-day city of the same name. Here, the fish god Dagon, originally a Canaanite deity, was worshiped in his own temple. The Ark, however, brought only trouble to its captors. The first calamity to befall the Philistines was the toppling of Dagon's image when the Ark was placed alongside him. The fact that the Philistines placed the Ark in their great cultic center shows that they held it in great reverence.

The shattering of their idol was followed by a plague of "emerods" thought to be bubonic plague, in the city and the surrounding area. The terrified Ashdodites lost no time in sending the Ark inland to Gath which commanded the entrance to the Valley of Elah on the borders of Israelite territory. Here too the plague broke out. In desperation, the Philistines sent the Ark to Ekron, the Philistine town nearest to the territory of Israel. It was from here that the Ark was returned to Israel, by the pass that led up to Beth-shemesh in the Judean foothills or Shephelah.

Unguided by human hand, two milking cows left their calves to pull a cart bearing the

The wanderings of the Ark among the Philistines.

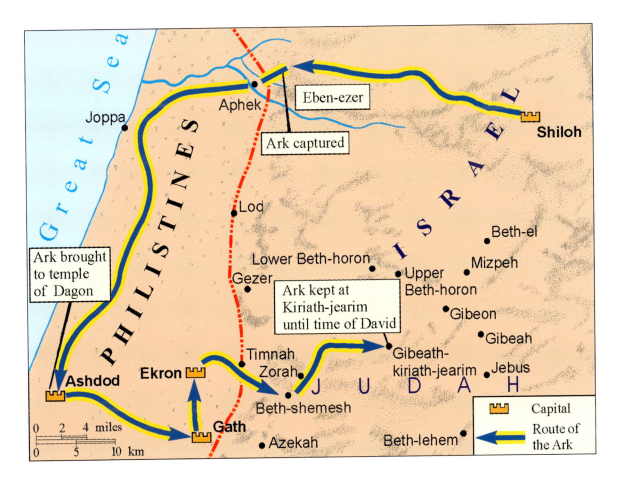

43

Ark behind them up the lush valley of Sorek. After seven eventful months the Ark had now left the land of the Philistines. Although the power of the Philistines and the necessity for strong opposition paved the way for the choosing of Israel's first king, Saul, by the tenth century BC, the rival settlers were almost completely assimilated into the local cultures.

They did however leave a lasting legacy in the name "Palestine," derived from Philistia and originally referring to the low-lying region under their control. During the Roman period, however, the term Palestine was extended from the coastal plain to include the whole land of Israel.

Clay figurine of a seated goddess, twelfth century BC, from Ashdod.

View of Beth Shemesh looking west through the Valley of Sorek. This view is taken from Tel Beth-shemesh, which is near the modern town of Beth Shemesh 12.5 miles (20 km) west of Jerusalem. If you examine an aerial photograph today, the way from Ekron (Tel Miqne) to Beth Shemesh stands out clearly. The biblical record says that "the kine took the straight way to the way of Beth-shemesh, and went along the highway..." (1 Sam. 6.12). The whole distance is a level plain.

The dip in the middle hill on the horizon marks the pass through which the Ark would have come after leaving Ekron. The Ark would then have passed by Timnah of the Philistines, where Samson found his first love (Judg. 14.1). Timnah has been identified with Tel Batash, a square-shaped mound in the alluvial Sorek plain, which is located just below the middle hill in the picture. A gate dating from this period has been found during recent excavations at this site. The road traveled by

the Ark must have passed by this massive entrance into the Philistine town.

The Ark was accompanied by the Philistine lords as far as "the border of Beth-shemesh," halfway between Beth-shemesh and Timnah. Up the broad valley full of ripened wheat it went, until it reached the field shown in this photograph.

Here on the southern bank of the valley, excavations of the ancient city of Beth-shemesh were begun in 1990, directed by S.

Bunimovitz and Z. Ledermann. The site had previously been excavated on behalf of the Palestine Exploration Fund in 1911–1912 and again by an American expedition in 1928–1933.

In the foreground, we see part of Area A of the most recent excavations where the remains of an Israelite building with a monolithic column which once supported a roof were found.

From Beth-shemesh to Kiriath-jearim

The Ark was not to remain at Beth-shemesh in the foothills, which was at this time disputed territory between the Philistines and the Israelites. Some of the men of Beth-shemesh, after their initial jubilation at the arrival of the Ark, failed to accord it proper respect, resulting in the destruction of 50,070 men. Reacting just like the Philistines, the terror-stricken Beth-shemites sought to rid themselves of the Ark's fearsome power: "Who is able to stand before this holy Lord God? and to whom shall he go up from us?" (1 Sam. 6.20).

The site of Kiriath-jearim was originally known as Kiryat el-Anab and in 1838 identified by Edward Robinson as the hill where the Ark was kept for twenty years after being brought up from Beth-shemesh (1 Sam. 6.1–2). Other sites vie for the same identification but this site with its remnant of the woods that are implicit in the name Kiriath-jearim ("Town of the Woods") has won general acceptance. One of the strongest points in its favor is its proximity to the other cities in the Gibeonite confederation to which it belonged (Josh. 9.17). These

View of Beth-shemesh looking east to the Judean Hills. Kiriath-jearim, visible in the far distance just to the right of the highest peak, was the nearest town in the hill country and although it belonged to the Gibeonites was in territory which was at that time conceded to Israel.

In the foreground, we see the remains of an ancient winepress cut in the rock where grapes were trodden. The surrounding area was noted for the cultivation of vines as the name of the valley, the Sorek (meaning "choice vine") indicates. The location of the great stone of Abel in the field of Joshua, where the Ark was placed and the two cows were sacrificed, is unknown. Mackenzie, the tel's first excavator, identified a rock terrace known as Wely Samson (Wely is Arabic for shrine) as this very stone.

Gibeonites are believed to have originated in Mesopotamia and to have formed themselves into a little republic in the Judean Hills. Joshua 9.17 lists their cities as "Gibeon and Chephirah and Beeroth and Kirjath-jearim."

The location of Kiryat el-Anab also suits the biblical description of Kiriath-jearim as on the border between Judah and Benjamin. In the allocation of the Land to the tribes, Joshua 15.9,60 include it in the portion given to Judah, while three chapters on, it is listed as one of the cities of Benjamin (Josh. 18.28). In this interesting fluctuation between Judah and Benjamin, Kiriath-jearim resembles Jerusalem, which is also variously described as belonging to one or the other tribe (Josh 15.63,18.28). This site is also easily accessible from the lowlands, where Beth Shemesh is located, via the passes through the dark limestone hills to the wooded ridge above.

The fact that it was a conspicuous high place (2,300 feet or 700 m above sea level) probably accounts for its former names Baalah, Kirjath-baal and Baale of Judah (Josh. 15.9, 18.14 and 2 Sam. 6.2). These probably refer to its use as a cultic site where ceremonies in honor of Baal took place.

Both in the story of the Ark's being brought to Kiriath-jearim and its removal by King David twenty years later (1 Sam. 7.1 and 2 Sam. 6.3, respectively), the detail that the house of Abinadab was on "the hill" (Hebrew, *geva*) is given prominence.

View of the hill of Kiriath-jearim, above the village of Abu Ghosh, about 8 miles (13 km) west of Jerusalem.

View of a floor identified as belonging to the house of Abinadab, just outside the basilica of Our Lady of the Ark of the Covenant, in Kiriath-jearim. The floor is plastered and some remains of mosaic have been preserved. A door sill is visible in the center of the photograph next to the seated boys. These remains would appear to be connected with the Byzantine church on whose foundation the modern church is built.

During the Ark's twenty-year sojourn on the hill, it was attended by a properly sanctified guardian, Eleazar, the son of Abinadab, in whose house the Ark was put for safe keeping. As the topography has barely changed in the last two thousand years, we can, in our mind's eye, picture the hill and the surrounding area with David and his thirty thousand chosen men who came to remove the Ark to its proper abode (2 Sam. 6.1–2).

The Byzantine church measured 92 by 59 feet (28 by 18 m) and had a central nave and apsis with two side aisles. Some monolithic columns of the atrium have been preserved, as have a number of column bases, capitals and mosaics.

The site is extraordinarily tranquil and is still maintained as a retreat center by the Sisters of Saint Joseph, drawing groups and individuals from within Israel and from all over the world. A recent archaeological survey, carried out because of a proposed building extension, has resulted in the site being renamed Tel Kiryat.

David bringing up the Ark from Kiriath-jearim, nineteenth century engraving.

Painting of King David before the Holy Ark, which adorns the walls inside the Church of Our Lady of the Ark of the Covenant in Kiriath-jearim. The harp-playing King David flanks the left side of the Ark while the High Priest with the censer of incense bows in reverence on the right. Six Levites (perhaps those that would bear the Ark) stand in the background singing. The Ark is manifested as a throne with the glorious manifestation of God (whose name, Yahweh, is written in Hebrew) between the Cherubim, which are beaten out of the mercy seat.

The twenty years that the Ark was secluded in Kiriath-jearim corresponded to the thirteen-year reign of Saul and the seven-year reign of David in Hebron (2 Sam. 5.5). All the time when David was fleeing and then reigning in Hebron, he dreamed of bringing up the Ark. One of the first things he did when he came to Jerusalem was to go to Kiriath-jearim intending to bring up the Ark to the city from which he now reigned over Israel. It may well be

that this beautiful painting attempts to express the fulfillment of David's desire, "Arise, O Lord, into thy rest; Thou, and the ark of thy strength, Let thy priests be clothed with righteousness; And let thy saints shout for joy" (Ps. 132.8–9).

He had long looked for "a place for the Lord, an habitation for the mighty God of Jacob" (Ps. 132.5). Now he had found it in the "fields of the wood" (v. 6). The fields of the wood, or in Hebrew *ya'ar*, of which *ye'arim* is the plural, appear to refer to the whole area around this lovely hill.

Looking toward Jerusalem

When David had the Ark of the Covenant removed from Kiriath-jearim, he did not follow the Scriptural stipulation that the Ark be carried by its staves on the shoulders of Kohathite priests. It was again placed on a cart driven by Ahio, son of Abinadab. The descent from the hill into the valley below is long but not steep. Next came a very steep ascent to a peak where the Crusader fortress of Castel now stands. This was followed by another descent into a fertile valley where the modern village of Motza is located. From there, the road climbs steadily up to Zion, the city that God had chosen, for "He hath desired it for his habitation" (Ps. 132.13).

But all did not proceed as planned. Somewhere between Kiriath-jearim and Jerusalem, they paid the price for the violation of the divinely prescribed procedure of transporting the Ark. At the threshing-floor of Nachon (2 Sam. 6.6 and 1 Chron. 13.9, where his name is given as Chidon) on the lower slopes of one of the rounded hills on the way, Uzzah, who presumably was guiding the cart while his brother drove it, touched the Ark in an attempt to steady it and was struck down instantly. This tragedy caused King David to change his mind about bringing the Ark up to the City of David. Instead, it was brought into a nearby house — again that of a Gentile.

Cart of Sea People drawn by oxen, from relief of Rameses III at Medinet Habu.

This view from Kiriath-jearim looking toward Jerusalem would have been the first view of the city gained by travelers coming from the coast before the construction of the new road in 1971. Mount Moriah, the hill on which the Temple was to be built under Solomon, David's son, was only slightly higher than Kiriath-jearim. It stood 2,428 feet (740 m) above sea level while Kiriath-jearim stands at 2,296 feet (700 m). The modern city of Jerusalem is silhouetted on the skyline. Today's Tel Aviv–Jerusalem highway, visible below in the valley, bypasses the village of Abu Ghosh.

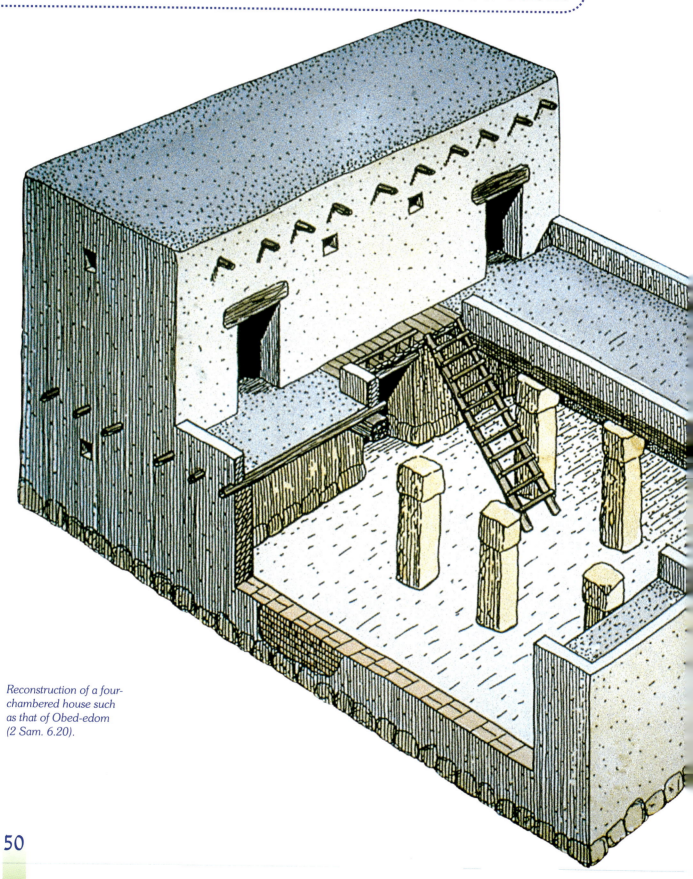

Reconstruction of a four-chambered house such as that of Obed-edom (2 Sam. 6.20).

The Scriptural account records that the Ark was carried "aside into the house of Obed-edom the Gittite" (2 Sam. 6.10). Now the name Obed-edom means "servant of man" but the remainder of his name implies that he came from the Philistine city of Gath, as did Goliath the Gittite (1 Chron. 20.5).

Achish the king of Gath had also granted refuge to David when he was fleeing from Saul (1 Sam. 27) and a band of six hundred Gittite fighting men followed David when he began his reign in Jerusalem (2 Sam. 15.18). One was Ittai the Gittite who, when he wanted to accompany David as he fled from Absalom, was reminded "thou art a stranger, and also an exile" (2 Sam. 15.19). This faithful man of Philistine origin was one of David's mighty men or "*gibborim.*"

The late Prof. Benjamin Mazar believed that "the quarter of the Gittites, including the house of Obed-edom, was located in Jerusalem, outside the City of David. This appears reasonable as the distance between the house of Obed-edom and the City of David does not, from the narrative in 2 Samuel 6.12–16, seem very far.

Again it is not certain how the Ark was kept for these twenty years in the house of a Gentile (2 Sam. 6.11). However, archaeological evidence reveals the type of house that prevailed throughout the country at that time. This house style had replaced the courtyard house of the earlier Bronze Age or Canaanite periods. It consisted of a three- or four-roomed house, usually rectangular in shape. It had one long space at the back and in the front, either two or three long parallel spaces built at right angles to the back space. The front spaces were often divided by rows of pillars. The houses usually had two stories. This typical four-room house was entered through an open court which had a roofed area on both sides supported by monolithic pillars. Livestock were usually kept in these sheltered areas while the roofs would have been used for drying fruit, etc. The back room may have served as living quarters but the main living area must have been on the second floor, which was secluded from the downstairs service area. We can only speculate as to where the Ark would have been stored, but it appears that the most likely place was in one of the roofed-over side spaces on either side of the courtyard. Perhaps one of the aisles (they were at least 16 feet or 5 m long) was cordoned off for the purpose. Because of the length of the staves, it is unlikely that the Ark could have been carried upstairs. However it was kept, the Ark stayed in a house such as this for twenty years and King David saw that its owner was blessed (2 Sam. 6.11, 1 Chron. 13.14).

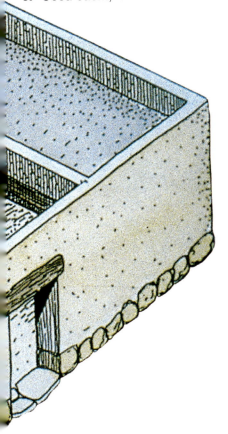

David and Solomon

The City of David

Although the Israelites had made attempts to take Jerusalem, it was only with David's victory over the Jebusites that they gained control over the city. Until then it was known as Jebus or the Stronghold of Zion (2 Sam. 5.7). During the long years of his flight from Saul and then his seven-year reign in Hebron, David longed for Jerusalem: "O send out thy light and thy truth: let them lead me; let them bring me unto thy holy hill, and to thy tabernacles. Then will I go unto the altar of God, unto God my exceeding joy: yea, upon the harp will I praise thee, O God my God" (Ps. 43.3–4).

The "holy hill" he referred to is the summit of Mount Moriah. Here Abraham had prepared to sacrifice Isaac (Gen. 22). After David's establishment of Jerusalem as his capital, the city would have been similar to the Jebusite city which preceded it. The area of the city remained confined to the lower slopes of the mountain, with the walls rebuilt over the earlier ones. The one striking difference would have been the massive royal palace in the northeast of the city. However, even this was based on an underlying foundation for a Jebusite citadel.

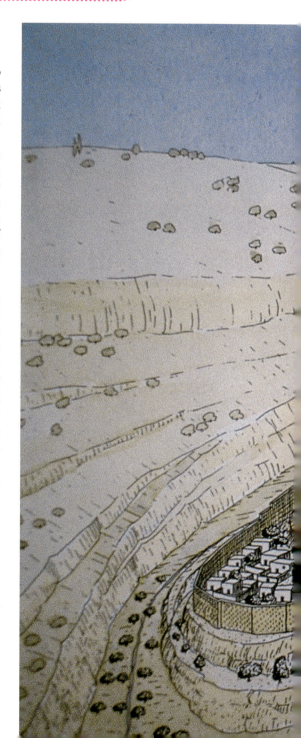

Reconstruction of the City of David. The city was located between the Kidron and Tyropoeon valleys and watered by the Gihon Spring that lay below the city gate. The palace was built to withstand attacks from the north. The place of the tent pitched by David to receive the Tabernacle is shown to the west (left in the photograph) of King David's palace.

Decorated fragment of a cultic stand found in Area G of the City of David, Iron Age.

The cedars of Lebanon, used to build the Temple.

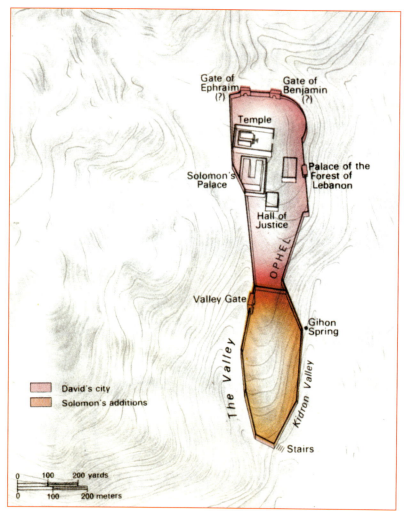

Map of Jerusalem at the time of David and Solomon.

View of what has been identified as the substructure of King David's palace in Jerusalem. Found in the excavations of the City of David, in Area G, by the archaeologist Yigal Shiloh, who died in 1987 at the age of 50. Having directed the dig from 1978 to 1982, Shiloh wrote: "The stepped stone structure in Area G is today one of the most impressive surviving monuments of the Iron Age in Israel, based on its size and state of preservation" (Yigal Shiloh, "Excavations at the City of David I, 1978–82," Interim report on the First Five Seasons, Qedem 19 [1984], p. 27). It consisted of a series of terraces filled with stones facing eastward and rising to the top of the slope. Shiloh believed that this massive structure had originally been created to allow the construction of

Abraham offering Isaac, nineteenth century engraving.

a Jebusite citadel and then strengthened and expanded by David as a foundation for his palace. Archaeologists Jane Cahill and David Tarler maintain that the entire structure was a single architectural unit constructed during the transition between the Late Bronze Age and Early Iron Age (thirteenth-twelfth centuries BC). If Shiloh is correct in identifying this structure as the base for David's palace, then the building must have been splendid indeed.

Scripture records that the stonework was built by the masons of Hiram the king of Tyre and that precious cedar wood worked by Phoenician carpenters was employed. The height of the original ground level can be seen from the marks of vegetation on the Hasmonean tower on the left.

The monument of King Hiram at Tyre.

King David's Palace and the Ark of the Covenant

Reconstruction of King David's palace with the tent for the Ark of the Covenant, looking southwest. This reconstruction is conjectural, but the palace could only have stood here on the summit of the hill occupying the site previously fortified by the Jebusites. The tent for the Ark is shown to the west (upper right in the drawing), as here there would have been sufficient space to accommodate large gatherings.

Scholars agree that David's palace could only have stood on the summit of the hill occupying the site previously fortified by the Jebusites. The Bible gives no details of the style of building used but we do know that the materials used in its construction, dressed building stones and cedar wood, were not in common use. No architectural remains firmly attributable to the palace have been found, but a number of fragments that would appear to derive from such a source have been discovered. The most notable of these is a capital of the proto-Aeolic type (thought to be developing towards the Greek Aeolic form), found in the excavations of Dame Kathleen Kenyon, the British archaeologist who excavated in the City of David from 1961 to 1967. The capital was found near Area G of Shiloh's excavations. Thirty-four such capitals have been found elsewhere in Israel at sites such as Dan, Ramat Rahel and Megiddo. As here in the City of David, none were found *in situ*, but all were discovered in the vicinity of large public buildings or palaces.

Also near Shiloh's Area G, Kenyon found ashlars, square blocks of hewn stone possibly

cut by Phoenician craftsmen, similar to those found by Shiloh himself, on the edge of this excavation area. In addition, a casemate wall, that is, a wall into which square compartments were built, dated to the tenth century BC, were found in Kenyon's Area H. These elements have all been incorporated into the reconstruction of David's palace. Proto-Aeolic capitals were used for the entrances and courtyard. Ashlars are the basic building blocks and the casemate wall protected the palace from the north.

It is conjectured that the tent for the Ark was to the west of the palace where there would have been sufficient space for large gatherings. There can rarely have been such a joyful occasion as the bringing up of the Ark into Jerusalem. Two whole chapters of the first book of Chronicles (15 and 16) are devoted to

its description. This time the Ark was carried by the staves on the shoulders of the Levites, as David said, "For because ye did it not at the first, the Lord our God made a breach upon us, for that we sought him not after the due order" (1 Chron. 15.13). The musical instruments that accompanied the singing Levites are carefully enumerated and so is the fact that the elders of Israel and the military captains were part of the procession. In fact, the record describes "all Israel" (1 Chron. 15.28) as involved in the ceremony. However, it is the picture of David's utter joy as expressed in his dancing that stands out in this account (also 2 Sam. 6.14–15). The Ark had now arrived at its last station before its installation in the Holy of Holies of the Temple built by Solomon, David's son.

Cult stand from Ashdod, c. tenth century BC, decorated with musicians playing the double pipe or horn.

Proto-Aeolic capital discovered in Kenyon's excavations in the City of David.

Singing Levites, nineteenth century engraving. "And David was clothed with a robe of fine linen, and all the Levites. . . . Thus all Israel brought up the ark of the covenant of the Lord with shouting, and with sound of the cornet, and with trumpets, and with cymbals, making a noise with psalteries and harps" (1 Chron. 15.27–28).

The City of Solomon

Reconstruction of the city of Solomon. The Temple is on the summit of Mount Moriah, with the Altar of David near the entrance to the east. The Temple and its court were the highest part of a complex of buildings which included the King's own house, the House of the Forest of Lebanon and the House of Pharaoh's Daughter, one of his wives. With this transfer of the royal complex, the stepped structure that supported David's citadel fell into disrepair. Just to the left of it, a path runs down to the shaft that led to the Gihon Spring (whose cave-like opening is visible outside the walls below the city gate). Excavations in the City of David have uncovered three segments of the Siloam channel which brought water from the Gihon Spring to a runoff pool at the southern end of the city. This channel was partly rock-hewn and partly stone-covered and can probably be identified with "the waters of Shiloah that go softly" mentioned in Isaiah 8.6. Apertures were cut in the rock face so some of this water could be diverted to irrigate the fertile tracts in the King's Vale below.*

Solomon had inherited a city that was not much more than a fortress. He left it a capital city, famed throughout the region for both its royal and religious significance. For the Ark, he built a Temple described as "exceeding magnifical" (1 Chron. 22.5), beside the altar built by David. The city served to centralize the tribes, drew on the wealth of the entire nation and enjoyed the revenues of the exotic trade developed by Solomon.

Solomon would have grown up seeing

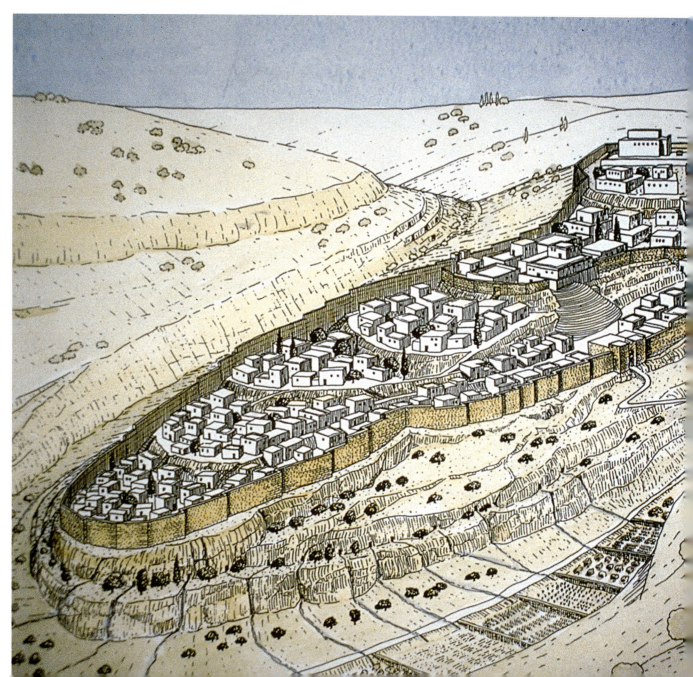

the tent in which the Ark was kept, aware that it could only be a temporary dwelling-place. He would also have seen the Altar built on the threshing-floor of Araunah the Jebusite and have heard that it was there that the terrible plague that affected the city was stopped. The last two chapters of 1 Chronicles detail the transfer from David to Solomon of the mission to build a "house of rest for the ark of the covenant of the Lord" (1 Chron. 28.2).

The Ark and the Tabernacle had been separated since the capture of the Ark by the Philistines. Solomon chose to inaugurate his reign by a visit to the high place of Gibeon where the Tabernacle was kept (1 Chron. 16.39). Endowed with the wisdom granted him there by God (2 Kings 3.12; 2 Chron. 1.12), he went "to sit upon the throne of the kingdom of the Lord over Israel" (1 Chron. 28.5).

Cross-section drawing of Warren's Shaft, showing one of the most ancient water supply systems in Jerusalem discovered in 1867 by Sir Charles Warren.

Nineteenth-century engraving of the Pool of Siloam.

Locating the earlier Temple platform (shown in yellow), which was only half the size of Herod's, involved a painstaking study of the ancient sources and the tracing of tell-tale clues on the present-day Temple Mount, where no excavation or proper survey is permitted. The tractate Middot in the Mishnah states that "the Temple Mount measured 500 cubits by 500 cubits" (*Middot* 2.1). This tractate was written after the Roman destruction in AD 70. However, Herod's extension of the Temple Mount was not considered holy by the rabbis and so their measurement referred specifically to the earlier Temple Mount.

The first clue to the earlier square platform was the peculiar angle of one of the steps at the northwest corner of today's raised platform. This step, while not parallel to the walls of the Moslem platform, is parallel to the eastern wall of the Temple Mount. This wall is unanimously considered to date from the period of the First Temple. Due to the steepness of the slope leading down to the Kidron Valley, Herod could not extend the platform on the east, but did so on the other three sides. This "step" is constructed of large bossed ashlars similar to those used in the central section of the ancient eastern wall. Its distance to the eastern wall

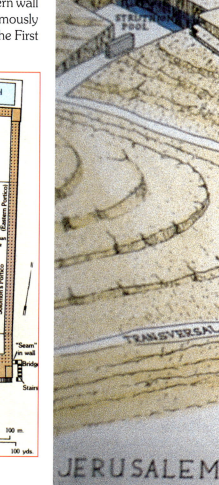

Plan of the Temple Mount during the Second Temple period.

turned out to be exactly 500 cubits using the royal cubit of 20.66 inches (525 mm). Confirmation that this was the northern line of the early Temple platform was found in the records of Sir Charles Warren who, during his explorations in this area, found a quarried rock-scarp in between the "cisterns" numbered 1 and 25 according to his numeration in the drawing. This quarried rock-scarp falls exactly on the line of the proposed northern wall and conforms with the necessity that the wall must run between the "step" and the deep fosse that lies just to the north.

Cutaway view of Mount Moriah with the walls of the successive temples shown in contrasting colors. The Rock, or Sakhra, which is the summit of Mount Moriah, is in the center. Twenty-two years of research led to the conclusion that the Temple must have stood on this spot. The rock mass with its underlying cave is clearly visible in the center of the picture and the spaces around it can be seen to conform to the description in Middot.

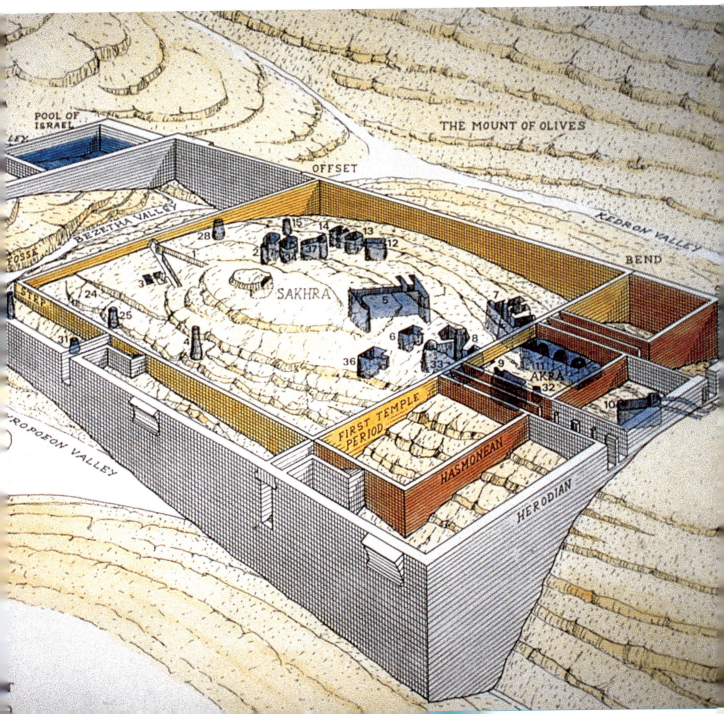

POOL OF ISRAEL

THE MOUNT OF OLIVES

OFFSET

KEDRON VALLEY

BEZETHA VALLEY

BEND

FOSSE

28

15 14 13

37 12

STEP

SAKHRA

5

7

24

25

31

6 8

36

33

9

AKRA

32

10

TYROPOEON VALLEY

FIRST TEMPLE PERIOD

HASMONEAN

HERODIAN

Measuring 500 cubits again from the proposed northeast corner brings us to a bend in the wall that had already been observed by Warren. The southern wall of the earlier Temple Mount was drawn by measuring 500 cubits from this "bend" parallel to the proposed northern wall. Many additional details tend to confirm this location of the 500-cubit square.

A Hasmonean extension to the Temple Mount which was made between the First Temple period and the Herodian (in about 141 BC) is shown in red. The location of the Akra, the fortress built by Antiochus Epiphanes in 186 BC has been found just to the south of the early Temple Mount, above the Cistern of the Akra, Cistern No. 11, according to Warren's numeration.

The Temple itself, according to *Middot*, was located inside the Temple Court, which measured 187 by 135 cubits. From additional measurements, the location of the Temple can be calculated. *Middot* 2.1 further informs us concerning the sizes of the courts which surrounded this Temple Court "the Temple Mount measured five hundred cubits by five hundred cubits. Its largest (open) space was to the south, the next largest to the east, the third largest to the north, and its smallest (open space) was to the west; the place where its measure was greatest was where its use was greatest."

Based on this information we may conclude that the Holy of Holies was located over the rock mass inside the Dome of the Rock, the Muslim shrine which now stands on this spot.

Plan of the Temple at Tell Tayinat, thought by scholars to be similar in structure to that of Solomon's Temple.

The water system on the Temple Mount, indicating the location of 37 water cisterns examined in the nineteenth century, mainly by Warren and Conder.

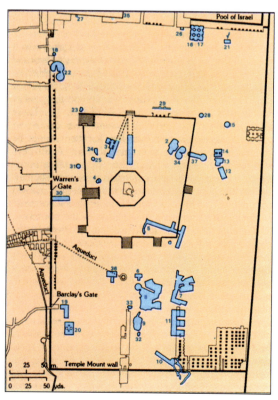

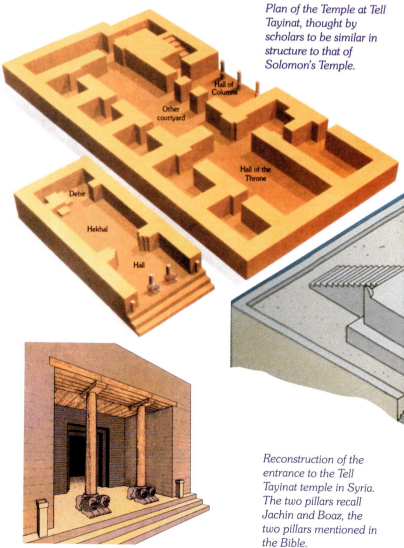

Reconstruction of the entrance to the Tell Tayinat temple in Syria. The two pillars recall Jachin and Boaz, the two pillars mentioned in the Bible.

Cutaway drawing of the Temple of Solomon, based on 1 Kings 6 and 7 and other biblical sources. The northern side of the Temple has been cut away to allow the details of the interior to be seen. The Temple measured 60 cubits long, 20 cubits wide and 30 cubits high (103 x 34 x 52 ft. or 31.5 x 10.5 x 15.75 m). In front of the Temple to the east stood the bronze Laver or Yam (Hebrew for "sea") which rested on twelve bronze oxen. These oxen were divided into groups of three, with each group facing the four points of the compass. This enormous basin which contained 2,000 "baths" of the biblical liquid measure, the equivalent of 16,000 gallons of water, was used by the priests in their ceremonial ablutions. On either side of the Temple

were five smaller lavers which rested on elaborate wheeled bases. Although no altar is described in the description of Solomon's Temple given in 1 Kings 7 and 8, an altar of brass is mentioned in passing in 1 Kings 8.64 and detailed in the other description of the Temple of Solomon in 2 Chronicles 4.1. Here it is recorded that it measured 20 cubits square and 10 cubits wide. This obviously differed from the Altar built by David but presumably stood in the same place over the threshing-floor of Araunah.

Three levels of chambers called "tselaot" or

bronze pillars are mentioned in connection with the Porch of the Temple. These were called Jachin (He shall establish) and Boaz (in him is strength) and in many representations are shown as free-standing columns. However, architectural reasoning and parallels to the Temple such as that at Tell Tayinat in Syria implies that their purpose must have been to support the Porch.

The Porch or Ulam stood in front of the Sanctuary and was 20 cubits long and 10 cubits wide. The description of the Temple in 2 Chronicles 3.4

The entrance through a wooden door would have given access to the Holy (or Heichal) which was 40 cubits long, 20 cubits wide and 30 cubits high. Here the walls were of cedar wood, carved with motifs of buds and open flowers. The floor was of fir wood overlaid with gold. Although in the Tabernacle, the Table of Shewbread stood on the north side, here both it and the Incense Altar are shown in the middle of the Holy. This is because the description of Solomon's Temple records five golden lampstands as standing on either side of the Holy.

The Holy was separated from the Most Holy by a partition made of olive wood carved with motifs of cherubim, palm trees and flowers overlaid with gold. A rocky ramp led up to the Holy of Holies, where the floor was

"yatsia" surrounded the Temple on three sides. The walls of the Sanctuary were built so that ledges were created on which the floors of these chambers could rest. Two

gives the height of this Porch as 120 cubits, which is a staggering 206 feet or 63 meters — the approximate height of a modern 21-story building! However, it may have been raised to this great height in the time of King Hezekiah. In the Temple built by Solomon, the Porch must have stood at least 30 cubits high if you add the height of the pillars and their capitals.

also of natural rock. The text of the English Bible reads as though the floor of the Holy of Holies was made of wood: "And he built twenty cubits on the sides of the house, both the floor and the walls with boards of cedar: he even built them for it within, even for the oracle, even for the most holy place" (1 Kings 6.16). In the Hebrew Bible, no floor is mentioned. A literal translation should read, "And he built twenty cubits from the sides of the house (the Holy) with boards of cedar from the ground until the walls and he built from the house, for the oracle, for the Holy of Holies."

The Final Resting Place of the Ark of the Covenant

The culmination of the journeys of the Ark of the Covenant was the installation of this holiest of objects in the Holy of Holies of Solomon's Temple. Solomon had spent seven years in building the Temple. When everything was ready, down to the smallest detail, "Then Solomon assembled the elders of Israel, and all the heads of the tribes, the chief of the fathers of the children of Israel, unto king Solomon in Jerusalem, that they might bring up the ark of the covenant of the Lord out of the city of David, which is Zion" (1 Kings 8.1). According to 1 Kings 8.4, the Tabernacle and all its vessels were brought into the Temple at the same time. We remember that the Tabernacle had been kept in Gibeon and there is no further mention of it in 1 Kings regarding the installation of the Ark into the Holy of Holies. A likely possibility is that the various places of the Tabernacle were stored in the chambers which surrounded the Temple. The Ark and the Tabernacle were

in a sense reunited but the Ark could now dwell in its permanent resting place.

When the Ark arrived at its final resting place, it was appropriate to remove the staves which represented its movable nature. "And they drew out the staves, that the ends of the staves were seen out in the holy place before the oracle, and they were not seen without: and there they are unto this day" (1 Kings 8.8). Thus the statement in Exodus 25.15 that the staves were not to be removed from the Ark must have applied to the time of its wanderings, which were now over. Also apparently ambivalent is the statement that "the ends of the staves were seen out in the holy place before the oracle" as opposed to "they were not seen without." We remember that in the Tabernacle the Holy of Holies measured 10 cubits long so that the length of the staves could not have measured more than this. The rectangular emplacement for the Ark

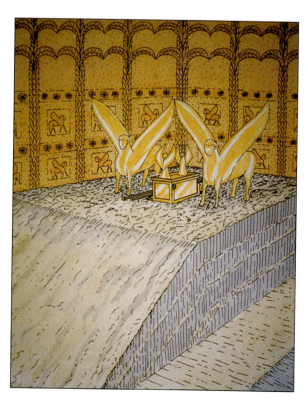

Drawing of the Ark of the Covenant in its resting place inside the Holy of Holies of Solomon's Temple. The Rock carried the whole of the Holy of Holies — therefore all of the Sakhra was the Foundation Stone or Even ha-Shetiyah. To the left, the southern wall is shown built on the Rock. The western wall (in background) was built against the natural scarp of the Rock while in the north (right side of the picture), the rock scarp was cut and a foundation trench created for the northern wall of the Holy of Holies.

A rocky ramp led up to the Holy of Holies from the east. The difference in height between the Holy and the Holy of Holies — the first was 30 cubits and the second 20 cubits — was partly taken up by this ramp, which was 5 cubits high. As the Holy of Holies was cubic in shape measuring 20 by 20 cubits, its roof was therefore 5 cubits lower than that of the Holy. The cube is an important shape in biblical symbology, i.e., the Holy of Holies in the Tabernacle and the city of Jerusalem in Revelation 21, and represents perfection.

The cherubim, drawn in outline form only to show that their depiction is speculative, are based on winged creatures which adorned representations of royal thrones from contemporary cultures and on Ezekiel 1.10 where an ox, a lion, a man and an eagle are mentioned in connection with the cherubim. The cherubim drawn here have the wings of an eagle, the face of a man, the front of a lion and the back of an ox.

that has been discovered shows that it stood in the center of the Holy of Holies. This meant that to remove the staves, the partition between the Holy and the Most Holy had to be opened and the ends of the staves were seen just before they were pulled out altogether. They would then have been placed down, presumably beside the Ark, and would no longer have been visible from "without."

We can only speculate on the appearance of the two large cherubim on either side of the Ark. Scripture records only that "the cherubim spread forth their two wings over the place of the ark, and the cherubim covered the ark and the staves thereof above" (1 Kings 8.7). In 2 Chronicles 3.10, we are told that they were made of "image work" overlaid with gold. Each of their wings was 5 cubits long which, when they were outstretched, filled the whole width of the Holy of Holies. Finally we are told in 2 Chronicles 3.13 that "they stood on their feet, and their faces were inward" (that is, toward the house or Holy). Every description of the cherubim given in the Bible is different.

The cherubim, the Ark and the decorations on the wall all remained unseen as "The Lord said that he would dwell in the thick darkness" (1 Kings 8.12). The ramp leading up into the Holy of Holies would have been climbed only once a year on the Day of Atonement, when the High Priest entered with his censer to sprinkle the blood of the sacrificial animals on the mercy seat. The cloud of the incense covered the mercy seat so that the priest would not be killed by the glory emanating from it.

From the biblical record it appears that the Ark remained in the Holy of Holies of Solomon's Temple until the reign of King Manasseh, who set a graven image of the *asherah* (or shrine) which he had made in the Temple (2 Kings 21.7; 2 Chron. 33.5). During the reign of Josiah we read that the king commanded the Levites to "Put the holy ark in the house which Solomon the son of David king of Israel did build; it shall not be a burden upon your shoulders" (2 Chron. 35.3). This would imply that the Ark had been removed for safe keeping by the Levites, very likely because of the sacrilege of Josiah's grandfather Manasseh. Following its restoration by Josiah, we hear no more of the Ark. There is no mention of it in the list of

Temple treasures carried off to Babylon when the city fell in 586 BC (2 Kings 25.13–17). Nor does it appear on the Arch of Titus in Rome, which depicts the triumphant procession of the Romans with the spoils of the Jerusalem Temple after its destruction in AD 70.

Seven-branched lampstand from relief on the Arch of Titus in Rome.

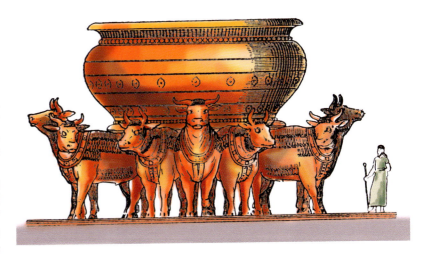

Conjectural representation of the "Sea of Solomon."

Relief on the Arch of Titus in Rome, depicting the triumphant procession of the Romans with the spoils of the Temple in Jerusalem after its destruction in AD 70.

The Temple Mount Today

The Dome of the Rock

The octagonal Dome of the Rock stands on the rocky summit of Mount Moriah. Visitors to the Muslim shrine, one of Jerusalem's best-known landmarks, can see the huge rock-mass of Es Sakhra (the Foundation Stone). The shrine was originally built by the Umayyad caliph Abd el Malik, between AD 688 and 691, and is the third holiest shrine in Islam after Mecca and Medina. Just prior to this the Caliph Omar, who took Jerusalem from the Byzantines in 638, had cleared the Rock which the Byzantine Christians had used as a dung heap to show that the site of the Temple was no longer relevant. For Muslims, the shrine commemorates the night journey of Mohammed who, they believe, ascended into Heaven from the rock on his winged steed El Burak. However, Muslims also have a tradition that here was the Kiblah (direction of prayer) of Moses as the Ark of the Covenant was placed on this rock.

The Rock is the highest point of Mount Moriah and tradition has it that the Sanctuary was located here. However, opinions differ as to whether it was the Holy of Holies or the Altar that occupied this spot. Placing the Altar over the Rock, which measures 43 feet by 56 feet (13 m by 17 m), would have caused the Rock to be completely buried since it is smaller than the Altar. Another problem with placing the Altar over the Rock would be that the well-known cave which lies below the Rock and which was supposed to have drained off the blood to the Kidron Valley, was in the wrong place. According to *Middot* 3.2, this original drain was located at the southwestern corner of the Altar, while the cave is in the southeast. An additional difficulty would be that if the Temple was built to the west of the Rock, its foundations would need to have been 50 feet (15.25 m) while, according to *Middot*, they were only 6 cubits (10 1/3 feet or 3.15 m) deep. The latest research has verified that it was indeed the Holy of Holies that stood over the Rock. As the Rock is also called the Foundation Stone or Even ha-Shetiyah (*Yoma* 5.2), this would truly be fitting.

Several texts in 1 Kings 6 and 8 may actually refer to a specially prepared place for the Ark. The First Book of Kings states that Solomon prepared the oracle "in the house within, to set there the ark of the covenant of the Lord" (v. 6.19) and in 1 Kings 8.6, "the priests brought in the ark of the covenant of the Lord unto *his* (or *its*) place, into the oracle (Dvir) of the house, to the most holy place, even under the wings of the cherubim." This means that a special place was prepared or assigned to the Ark. This is further emphasized in verses 20–21 of the same chapter, where Solomon says that he has "built an house for the name of the Lord God of Israel. And I have set there a place for the ark." The Hebrew verb "*seem*" (שים), which is translated here as "set," can also mean "put" or "make." In the light of this discovery we suggest to translate this verse as "I have made there a place for the Ark."

(opposite) View of the Dome of the Rock.

Artist's rendering of the High Priest.

View of the pitted and scarred surface of the Rock inside the Dome of the Rock. The photograph was taken from the ambulatory or walkway below the dome from where there is a good vantage point. Visitors usually view the rock from behind a high wooden fence, which makes looking at details difficult.

Beginning a careful analysis of the Rock, two flat rectangular areas on the southern side of the Rock (left in the picture) were detected. These were familiar as foundation trenches created when the rock had been leveled to make flat bases for square or rectangular foundation stones. Without cutting a foundation trench, the stones would have wobbled about so that the building would not have been safe.

Putting these foundation trenches together with other flat areas adjoining them on the south (difficult to discern in the photograph) it looked as though this was the base for a broad wall that would have run from east to west. The thickness of this wall is over 10 feet (3 m) from north to south. As this coincided with the measurement given in Middot for the thickness of the walls of the Second Temple — 6 cubits (10.3 feet or 3.15 m) — the conclusion that

here had stood the southern wall of the Holy of Holies was inescapable.

Turning to the western side of the Rock (top in the picture), we saw that this edge was a natural rockscarp. We then noted that the direction of this scarp is virtually identical to that of the eastern wall of the Temple Mount whose line had remained unchanged. It appeared reasonable to deduce that the western wall of the Holy of Holies stood against this

rockscarp. The distance from the southern wall of the Holy of Holies to the northern edge of the Rock is exactly 20 cubits (the measurement for one of the sides of the square Holy of Holies of the Temple—1 Kings 6.20). The northern wall of the Holy of Holies would have been built exactly here, at the foot of the northernmost scarp, which was cut originally for this purpose. We had now determined the location of three of the walls of the Holy of Holies.

There was never a stone wall between the Holy of Holies (or Dvir) and the Holy (also called Heichal) and therefore no foundation trench would have been visible on the sloping surface in the east of the Rock. Nevertheless, on plan, we can plot the division line between the two chambers of the Sanctuary, so that the whole area occupied by the Holy of Holies can be set out.

View of the Rock showing the location of the Holy of Holies. On the left is the foundation trench for the southern wall of the Holy of Holies. The western scarp measures 20 cubits, as did each side of the Holy of Holies. The northern scarp had originally been cut to fit these measurements. The partition between the Holy of Holies (Dvir) is indicated by a broken line.

Two distinctive depressions are visible, almost side by side in the northern part of the rock. The southernmost of these (on left in the photograph) is an apparently artificially cut trapezoid indentation with two ledges spreading out toward the west. In the deepest point, no rock is visible, only small stones and mortar. It has been suggested that this place may be of special importance as the planting place for a tree for Ashera. However, as this place is located at the very center of the Dome of the Rock, it may have played a role as the central pivot from which the plan of the Dome of the Rock was set out on the ground for its construction.

Just to the north of this is a rectangular depression, the sides of which have an estimated height of 0.5 to 6 inches (1 to 15 cm). The identification of this depression proved to be the most moving part of the entire research. Although we had not gone looking for a sensational find, but had simply homed in from the exterior walls of the Temple Mount on the interior of the Temple itself, the location of this feature pointed to its identification as the former resting-place of the Ark of the Covenant. According to this plan, it falls exactly in the center of the Holy of Holies. The dimensions of this level basin agree with those of the Ark of the Covenant which were 1.5 cubits (2 ft. 7 in. x 4 ft. 4 in. or 79 cm x 131 cm), with the longitudinal axis coinciding with that of the Temple. It appears therefore that during the First Temple period a special place was prepared for the Ark by cutting this flat basin in the rock. It is clear that without such a flat area the Ark would have wobbled about in an undignified manner, which would not conceivably have been allowed.

Apart from the depressions mentioned above, many cuts were made in the Rock during the period of Crusader domination of the Temple Mount when the Christians built a church called Templum Domini over the Rock. The cuts visible on the eastern slope of the Rock are the result of a Crusader practice of raising money by selling pieces of the rock for their weight in gold.

WEST SCARP
20 CUBITS

NORTH SCARP

FOUNDATION TRENCH

RECTANGULAR DEPRESSION

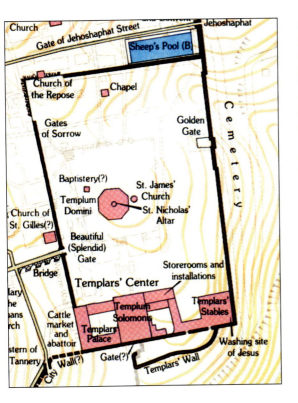

The Temple Mount in the Crusader period, 1099–1187.

Cross section of the Temple Mount from east to west. This section shows clearly that the Rock is the highest point of the Mount. The Tyropoeon Valley lies to the west (left in the drawing) and the descent to the Kidron on the east (right in the drawing).

The Muslim platform and buildings, the Dome of the Rock, and the Dome of the Chain are shown in blue. Herod's Temple and its courts, the Altar and the Nicanor Gate are indicated in red. As Herod's Temple was a renewal of the previous one, there is no reason to believe that it was built in a different place, so we shall first examine indications of this Herodian Temple and then see how this differed from the Temple of Solomon.

Clearly visible in this section is the 6-cubit-high foundation built for Herod's Temple (Middot 4.6), which almost completely buried the Rock. It also shows that the present-day Muslim platform is lower than the foundations of Herod's Temple and proves that not only was the Temple destroyed but that most if not all of the foundation was also removed. The massive size of Herod's Temple is also apparent in comparison to the Dome of the Rock — it stands 1.5 times as high as the Muslim shrine. The Dome of the Chain stands on the place occupied by the Porch of Herod's Temple and the steps leading up to it. To the east of the Dome of the Rock, the present-day platform is higher than the area where the Altar, the Courts of the Priests and that of the Israelites were located. According to Middot 5, the location of the Altar can be calculated to have been 21.6 feet (6.6 m) east of the Dome of the Chain, leaving the possibility of some remains surviving there, such as parts of the base of the Altar, the channel through which the blood was drained to the Kidron Valley, the pavements and steps of the courts.

The section also shows that the Rock could not have been the site of the Altar as this would move the Temple so far to the west as to be incompatible with the record that the foundation was 6 cubits high. It would also make the back wall of the Temple coincide with the western wall of the 500 cubit square and would leave no room for a western Temple court. The converging lines of vision to the top of the Mount of Olives are indicated, proving that the door of the Sanctuary could be seen through the Nicanor Gate, fulfilling the requirement in the Mishnaic tractate (Para. 3.9; 4.2) that the High Priest performing the sacrifice of the Red Heifer (Num. 19.1–10) should be able to look directly into the Sanctuary entrance from the Mount of Olives.

It is obvious that the level of Solomon's Temple was lower as it did not have the 6-cubit foundation that Herod's did. Solomon's Temple had a wooden floor laid directly above the natural bedrock which is visible in the section. When the Ark was brought into the Most Holy, the priests would walk over such a floor in the Holy and climb the rocky ramp that led up to the Holy of Holies.

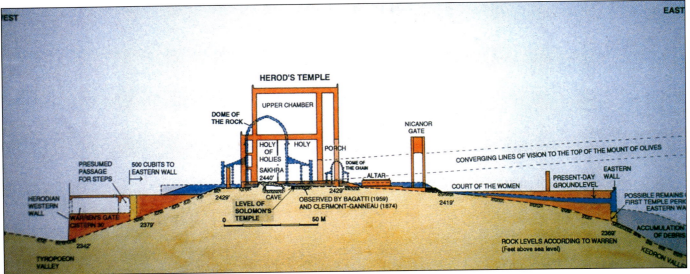

Conclusion

The finding of the site of the Ark of the Covenant, so wonderfully preserved despite all the assaults the rock had undergone, was a most felicitous conclusion to twenty-two years of research on the Temple Mount.

In recent years, there has been a surge of interest in finding the actual Ark of the Covenant. According to the Second Book of Maccabees (2.1–8), Jeremiah hid the Ark on Mount Nebo in Jordan. Others would place it as far afield as Axum in Ethiopia or Tara in Ireland. Many rabbis, on the other hand, believe that the Ark is hidden somewhere beneath the Temple Mount.

Nobody knows where the Ark of the Covenant is.

However, Divine solicitude towards this holiest of objects may extend beyond its recorded history. The account in Numbers 3, which deals with the responsibilities of the various Levitical families concerning the Tabernacle, gives the name of the chief of the Kohathites, the first person ever to have been in charge of the Ark of the Covenant, as Elizaphan ben Uzziel (verse 30). His name means "My El (God) has hidden" and he was the son (ben) of "My Strength is El." It is a comforting thought that if the Ark exists, it is hidden with the knowledge of God himself and will be found when it suits Him best.